SONGWEAVER

An astonishing friendship.

A cascade of mysteries.

LOST

A snarl of secrets.

And a couple steps
away from disaster.

Songweaver Lost

David E. Gaston

Canterbury
Studios

Edited by Sarah Beach

Cover design and illustrations © 2023 by Carrie Gaston

Published by Canterbury Studios, Reseda, California

1st edition 2023

Visit us at davidegaston.com

Library of Congress Control Number: 2023916392

ISBN: 978-0-9617934-0-1 ebook

ISBN: 978-0-9617934-1-8 paperback

* * *

For Carrie

* * *

Chapter 1

The Hollow Between the Hills

WAITING ALONE in the shade of an oak tree for the morning school bus, Jessica Blackwater realized she was already angry.

She blew some air through her lips and wiped away a few stray hairs and muttered "*This stinks*" under her breath. The anger itself didn't bother her all that much—she'd gotten used to it, recently—but the timing couldn't have been worse. It put her off balance just when she needed to get her head straight, before heading off to school where the real trouble waited.

She craned her neck and shaded her eyes, straining to see the bus and wondering when the anger had actually started, this time. The answer came quickly enough: last evening at the dinner table, when Jessica's mother had tried to talk to her about her father. The man had abandoned the two of them last year, packing his suitcases and moving to Florida and divorcing Jessica's mother after he got there. The break came after ragged years of lies, insults, and drunken arguments—even now the memories balled up Jessica's fists and made her breathe through gritted teeth. But for reasons Jessica could not fathom her mother kept making excuses for him. She said that her father still loved her ("in his own way") and he'd left a message

1

and sent a card for Jessica's twelfth birthday last week, and she could totally understand if Jessica didn't want to talk to him, but it might help if she just *tried*, just read one of his notes or called him on the phone.... Jessica made a brief attempt at saying that she would never again believe anything the man said and probably never speak to him for the rest of her life— but it only left her mother looking surprised and hurt. Jessica broke off the conversation and went to her room and shut the door. It was better than yelling.

So, in a nutshell: she was angry with her father for being an abusive manipulating jerk (as usual) and angry with her mother for being unbelievably oblivious about it (that part was new) and angry with herself for upsetting her mother when it wasn't even her fault.

Awesome, she thought. *I've reached anger nirvana. And it's not even 8:00 a.m.*

She tapped a foot on the ground and drummed her fingers on a leg, wishing the bus would hurry. But now she began to wonder why she was in such a rush. On warm September days like this one the bus smelled foul inside, like diesel fumes and old chewing gum, and kids would be laughing and cracking jokes, and when they saw her frustration they'd make her a target, hoping she'd yell at them and get in trouble with the driver....

Almost without thinking Jessica stepped away from the bus stop and started down the road. She had walked to school on other days but never without planning ahead. "I shouldn't do this," she muttered. "I'll just be late, or sweaty or tired." But she didn't stop.

She followed the concrete sidewalk as the road took a long sweeping curve through the tail end of her housing tract. Not far beyond the last house the walkway gave way to bare dirt. The main road now ran alongside a broad field, thick with dry grasses and the husks of wildflower plants, crisped and yellowed after the long summer. In the small valley where Jessica lived there were many open areas like this one, wild-looking spaces between the clusters of homes. They almost made her feel that she lived out in the country, though the big cities of Southern California were only a few miles away.

Further along she came to a dirt road veering off to the right through the field; it was her shortcut to the school. Within a few minutes the sounds of tires and auto engines fell away behind her. She began to hear insects buzzing in the tumbleweeds and birds chirruping in a pale-skinned sycamore that shadowed the path. Ahead she could see the hills that marked the border of the valley, the yellow grasses on their slopes riffling like water in the breeze. Jessica inhaled the fresh air and felt her head start to clear.

The walking had relaxed her but it also gave her time to think, which wasn't actually helpful. Because she had another reason for feeling upset—

No, she thought. *Don't go there.*

Last night in her bed she had turned to the wall and pressed a hand against it, as she often did, trying to imagine the sounds her older brother Brad used to make in the next room. On nights when she couldn't sleep she pretended she could still hear the floorboards creaking as he walked around, or his drumsticks tapping as he practiced on book covers or the back of a chair—

I told you, don't go there, it won't help.

He had run away nearly two years ago in the middle of the night after a horrible fight with their father. Out of everything Jessica had lived through, nothing had been worse than losing her brother. She didn't blame Brad for leaving, she knew he had to do it, but he'd said nothing to her. Not even goodbye. He'd made their home almost bearable when she was younger but now she didn't even know if he was still—

How many times do I have to say it? Just shut it down! I can't fix it and it only hurts to drag it up....

With the argument running in her head Jessica hardly noticed as the dirt road reached the base of the hills and climbed a slope to a low saddle. Here the summer sun had baked the earth as hard as concrete and the road was littered with rabbit droppings. Just as she crested the ridge and began descending, she heard someone playing a flute.

At least it sounded like a flute, or possibly a recorder. She turned to look back, expecting to see a bicyclist or a jogger with a music player; but there were no bikes or people anywhere in sight. In a few moments the music dropped below a whisper and faded away.

Okay—kinda weird, she thought, as she continued down the slope. The track slipped down and crossed a hollow between two hills before rambling along a ravine back to a civilized street. When Jessica reached the hollow she heard the music again. There was no mistaking it now: it came from the left, through a thicket of tall dry plants.

She wondered if she should just walk away quietly; a piper practicing in such a lonely place might not welcome a visitor. But now that she heard the tune clearly she found it too interesting to ignore. She took cautious steps through the first few plants and parted the last of them with both hands.

Lying on a sandy spot of ground was a young barefoot girl. She lay on her back, one leg crossed over a raised knee, toes bouncing with the beat. Her musical instrument looked like several wooden tubes bound together, small enough to hold to her lips but large enough to have a few finger holes. (The word *panpipes* popped into Jessica's head, but she wasn't sure it was correct.) The music sounded beautiful but somewhat aimless. Jessica thought she'd begun making sense of it just as it stopped; the girl had turned to look at her.

4

Jessica blinked. "Oh, sorry...I didn't mean to interrupt. Just wondered where the music was coming from...."

The girl sat up. "You heard it!" she said. "You heard me playing, didn't you?"

"Well...yeah, sure. You're good at it."

The girl stared at her. She seemed about ten years old and her eyes looked green in the sunlight. She was wearing blue jeans cut off at the knees and a greenish shirt a few sizes too large, and her dark hair stuck out in various directions around her face. She kept staring but didn't speak.

Jessica said, "Well...okay. I have to get going," as she backed out through the plants. The girl got up to follow. When they came to the road she walked up uncomfortably close and looked up into Jessica's face (the girl was at least a few inches shorter). Jessica had no idea what to say; she was almost ready to run.

The girl said, "Do this." She stuck out her tongue, the end of it curled into an 'O.'

Jessica stared and sputtered a laugh. "Okay," she said, and curled her tongue (some people have trouble with this, but it came easily for Jessica). Then she said, "Can you do this?" and flipped the end of her tongue over to the right. The girl stared at her wide-eyed and put her face through painful-looking contortions.

"No! No!" she laughed, dancing in a circle. "I can't do it! I can't!"

Jessica laughed along with her. "You're crazy, you know? What's your name?"

"Ariel," the girl said. "Do this." She made an odd twisting movement with one arm. Jessica frowned and tried to copy the movement, and after a few attempts she thought she managed it fairly well.

"Yes! Good! Now listen." The girl played a short tune on her pipes, a melody almost liquid with trills and runs. She closed the piece with a flourish and said, "What did you see?"

"Umm...what did I *see*?" Jessica wrinkled her nose. "I was thinking of a creek, I guess. A slow creek, with lots of round pebbles on the bottom—"

"Wonderful! And trees! Did you see them?"

"Umm...yeah. Willow trees. And one of them had branches trailing in the wa—"

"Yes! Yes! Yes!" Ariel danced and clapped and Jessica laughed again. The girl was certainly strange but she seemed happy about almost everything, and the feeling was infectious.

Ariel ran up to her and grabbed her hand. "I want to see you again. Tomorrow! Can you be here? Say you'll come, please!"

"Sure, I can be here," Jessica said. "It's no problem."

"Good! Don't be late!" And then she spun around on one heel and vanished.

Jessica blinked at the swirl of dust. It certainly *looked* as though Ariel had disappeared like a soap bubble popping in the air, but Jessica was practical enough to know that it had to be some kind of trick. "Hey, that was pretty good! How'd you do that?" she called. She poked through the shrubs beside the road. "Are you a magician or something? Come on out, I want to talk to you!" She went back to the clearing where she had first seen the girl and found it empty. About ten yards down the road was a large rock; she climbed it and looked all around the hollow, scanning the hillsides and calling out. No one answered.

Jessica frowned at the air. *Well, this is just...weirder and weirder. And ridiculous. And one more thing I didn't need today.* A part of her wanted to stay and figure out what had happened; another part had calculated how much further she had to walk and was annoyingly pointing out that any more delays would likely make her late for school. She brushed dust off of her jeans, grumbling, and set off down the road.

With all the thoughts crossing in her head she didn't pay much attention to the path, but her feet seemed to manage well enough on their own. Twenty minutes after leaving the hollow she looked up and saw that she'd arrived at the school. A crowd of students, a hundred or more, had gathered in the plaza in front of the gate, chatting in groups or texting or talking on cell phones. Jessica felt her stomach twist at the sight; it was the worst possible time for her to get there. She drifted off to the side near one end of the stainless-steel arch over the gate, an assemblage of rods and shards that supposedly formed the initials JCECAPE though Jessica had never been able to make them out.

The full name of the place was *The Julius C. Esterhaus Center for Academic and Personal Enrichment*, or Esterhaus for short. It was a rather exclusive private academy that seemed to be popular with parents who worked in the film and music businesses in Los Angeles. Under normal circumstances, with no family background and her mother's income barely keeping them fed, Jessica never would have set foot on the school grounds. But back in January Esterhaus had announced a program called "Good Neighbor: A Vision for 1998" that aimed to "proactively engage with the less-advantaged in our local community." Jessica's mother had spent long evenings and weekends attending meetings and filling out forms in order to win her daughter one of the handful of openings. And that was why Jessica was afraid to tell her that she really, really didn't want to be there and would much rather be at the public school near their home.

Over at the curb, cars driven by chauffeurs were stopping to drop off more students. The girls getting out of those cars wore tailored outfits from designers Jessica had probably never heard of and hairstyles that looked as though they had spent the morning at a salon. For her part, Jessica was wearing baggy jeans and a shirt (she almost always wore baggy jeans and a shirt) and she had brushed her hair back from her forehead (she almost always brushed it back). She slid a little further into the shadow of the arch.

The first bell rang. In singles and small clusters the crowd began breaking up and moving through the gate. Jessica tried to mingle unobtrusively. As the space narrowed she accidentally jostled a girl talking with some friends.

"Sorry," she said.

"Don't scuff my shoes, Kmart," the girl said, hardly glancing in her direction. They called her "Kmart" because of her clothes.

Inside the front gate a covered walkway led across a grassy area to the central quad. Even though people packed the walkway almost side-to-side, four or five boys came rushing up from behind, shouldering through the crowd as though running a race. One of them stumbled hard against Jessica's back, almost slamming her into a metal post.

"No fair!" the boy yelled to his friends. "I tripped on a short-bus!" Any of the local kids who rode the school bus in the morning were called "shortbus."

Jessica picked herself up, fighting back the retorts that burned in her throat, and kept walking. Another boy called out "Smooth move, scrub," and Jessica figured he was probably talking to her, but she didn't bother to find out. Scrub was short for "scrubface," a term for any girl who didn't wear makeup.

As the crowd spilled out into the central quad, people began separating to walk to their classes in the various school buildings. Jessica slipped to the side behind a square pillar supporting one of the odd-looking artworks that dotted the Esterhaus campus. She leaned back against the stone and took a breath.

Okay, not so bad today, she thought. People called her

"Kmart" on her better days. On the bad days it was usually "Goodwill."

As she settled herself, she heard her friend Mitch Carlucci running up the walkway. She knew it was Mitch from the clumping sound his sneakers made as they slapped on the concrete (he was rather flat-footed).

Mitch poked his head around the corner of the pillar. "Hey, Jessie, you OK? I thought I saw you trip or something."

"Well, it was more of a shove than a trip," Jessica said. "But I'm OK."

"Cool. I wasn't sure you'd be here, I didn't see you on the bus." Mitch lived in Jessica's neighborhood and his parents couldn't afford Esterhaus any more than Jessica's mother. But he'd gotten enrolled on an academic scholarship—at twelve years old. He was brilliant, though you couldn't tell by looking at him.

"Yeah, I decided to walk today," she said. "On short notice."

"Oh, right. You should show me that route you take, I don't see how you can get here on time."

"It's not hard. You know the dirt road, through the field...." She trailed off. "Look, something weird happened this morning —*really* weird. You're not gonna believe it."

"Oh, yeah?"

"I'll tell you the whole thing but not now. You'll be home after school?"

"Yeah, I'll be practicing. Come over whenever you want."

Jessica made several attempts to actually pay attention in her classes that day, without much success. Even on days with few distractions she never found it easy to focus on schoolwork at Esterhaus. It wasn't exactly an ordinary sort of school.

The teachers there didn't act like any teachers Jessica had ever seen. Many said they didn't like the word *teacher* because it was too "second-wave" (which meant something like old-fashioned). They preferred to be called *discovery coordinators*. And instead of having classes they had *freeform interactions*. Some of them even avoided using schoolbooks, because printed words "tended to stifle the natural learning process."

In Jessica's first class that morning—"Personal Geography" —the teacher (everyone called him Mike) walked in a few minutes late and dropped a stack of old vinyl record albums on the desk. He was wearing aviator-style sunglasses and faded blue jeans with holes in the knees. "Okay, campers," he said, "time to get serious." He yanked a wall map of the United States down from its canister and then sat on the edge of the desk. "You guys all know where the Pacific Ocean is, right? It's the big mess of water out there when you go to the beach." A few people chuckled briefly. "And the ocean is important for all of us. It makes the nice weather around here, gives us those cool breezes. And in the summer we can all go there and cool off, hang out with friends, whatever."

Mike got up and started pacing the front of the room. "But suppose—just suppose—the ocean wasn't there anymore. Wouldn't that be crazy? No more breezes. No more boats. No place to fish. And get this: no waves for surfing."

A murmur arose from some of the students; one of them muttered, "Bogus."

"You got it," Mike said. "All right, everyone get out some paper. I want half a page on 'What My Summer Would Be Like If the Pacific Ocean Disappeared.'"

That class was rather typical of Jessica's time at Esterhaus. She'd started her second year at the place still trying to figure out what exactly the teachers expected her to do. She rarely felt she'd learned anything during a school day; the only thing that seemed to matter was being inventive or different in some way. Unfortunately, most of the time, Jessica didn't feel very creative. She'd never had much talent for art and didn't enjoy inventing stories. She was reluctant to say it, but a lot of what happened at the school just seemed silly. It made her wonder if something was wrong with her brain.

During her first year there had actually been a class she enjoyed very much: Modern European History, taught by Mr. McNulty. He looked older than most of the other teachers and no one ever called him by his first name (which was George). The way he talked about history made Jessica feel that it might be important after all. She'd been fascinated by the French Revolution and still had a vivid picture in her mind of Napoleon Bonaparte and Czar Alexander of Russia, when they met together on a raft in the middle of a river and divided the whole world between the two of them. But not many other students seemed to enjoy the class. They acted surprised when Mr. McNulty assigned books and expected them to read them, or assigned homework and expected them to turn it in.

Before long Jessica heard students grumbling, saying things like "He's just teaching us facts." Jessica wasn't sure why this was a criticism but people began taking it seriously. Soon parents were complaining to other teachers and teachers were shaking their heads in the hallways, murmuring about "outdated learning concepts" and the need for the whole staff to "share the Esterhaus vision." Eventually even the principal told people that "maybe George would be happier somewhere else."

All this time no one bothered to say anything directly to Mr. McNulty, and nothing came of it until late in the semester, when he sent letters to about half of his students telling them that they were likely to fail unless their work improved. On Friday of that week the principal invited Mr. McNulty in for a chat; on the following Monday Jessica heard that her teacher had taken "an early retirement." A substitute took over the class and they spent the rest of the semester watching classic movies from France and Germany.

· · ·

11

The end of the school day came along in its own good time, quite a bit later than Jessica would have liked. She took the bus home as usual and the ride was uneventful.

From the bus stop she walked past the oak tree at the corner and then around a turn into her own street. Her home was the third on the left, a small boxy townhouse on a street lined with small boxy townhouses. When four people lived there it had sometimes felt narrow and cramped, but it was more than large enough for just two. Jessica let herself in with her own key. The rooms were empty—her mother wouldn't be home for another three hours. Jessica ignored the silence as she changed clothes, then left the house and walked to Mitch's place.

Mitch was already practicing basketball in his driveway, dribbling and taking shots at the hoop over the garage door. Seeing her he called, "Hey, Jessie! Watch, this is new!" He dribbled to one side and looped a hook shot over his head. The ball arched high and caromed off the side of the rim.

"Ah, shoot!" he said. "I made that just yesterday. One more try." He threw up another hook, this time missing the backboard and banging the ball against the wall of the garage. Jessica caught it on the bounce and tossed it back to him, saying, "Listen, Mitch, I want to tell you what happened—"

"One more minute." He bounced the ball to the bottom of the driveway and grabbed it with both hands. "He's got the ball at midcourt," he called. "Three seconds, two seconds...he shoots!" He heaved a shot that hit to the right of the basket and bounded into the street.

"Wow, almost in!" he said. "I'm gonna make one of those someday, I just know it."

Jessica ran after the ball and brought it back. There wasn't much point in talking to Mitch until he made a couple baskets, so she stood to one side and caught the ball when it flew that direction.

Mitch was odd in some ways and Jessica liked that about

him. You could see part of the oddness by looking in his eyes: they were different colors, the right one blue and the left hazel-colored, brown with streaks of green. Jessica barely thought about it now but she'd noticed a common reaction when people met him: they would peer at his face and then turn away, as though they wanted to stare but didn't want to get caught.

Mitch would say helpfully, "It's called *heterochromia iridis*—just means your eyes are different colors. Almost 1% of people have it. Not as rare as you'd think."

The other odd thing was that he was easily the smartest person Jessica had ever met, but he either hadn't noticed this or just didn't care. His mind seemed to retain every idea that came near him and he absorbed math and science like other people read comic books. In a normal world he would probably end up researching physics or designing satellites or computers. But whenever someone asked what he wanted to do with his life he would say, "I'm going to be a basketball player." And even Jessica, who rarely played sports, could see that he was too slow, couldn't jump, and got the ball in the basket about as often as it rained in August.

Jessica's mother once told her that some people get bored with things that come easily and only get interested in things they can't do. She supposed that might be a good description of Mitch.

Eventually a couple of shots went in and Jessica applauded, and Mitch sat on the ground out of breath. "That was great!" he said. "I'm getting so I can make layups half the time, almost. Now, what did you say?"

Jessica sat beside him and told the whole story. By the time she finished he was staring at her sideways with his eyes narrowed and his mouth half-open.

"You're kidding me. Are you kidding me?" he said.

"Not a bit," she said.

"She vanished, just like that?"

"Just like that."

"No way."

"I'm totally not making it up," Jessica said. "And you know I'd just look stupid if I told anyone else."

Mitch snorted and bounced the ball between his legs. "What was that stuff about curling your tongue? And the thing with the trees and the water?"

"I have *no* idea."

"Yeah—okay. So, what do you really think?"

Jessica wrinkled her nose. "Well, there's got to be an explanation, right? I mean, it's just ridiculous. People can't do that, right?"

They stared at each other, then smiled at the same time. They leaned closer as Mitch said, "But what if she did? What if she really did?"

"It would be so *great*," Jessica said. "I would fall apart. I would die."

"It'd be magic," he said. "No, bigger than that. It would be like...something from a cartoon, like Scooby-Doo or those Japanese anime shows."

"Uh-huh. You know what I thought, who Ariel's really like? Pippi Longstocking."

"Yeah. Or Peter Pan."

"But Peter Pan was a boy."

"Yeah, but did you know when they do 'Peter Pan' on stage, they always have a girl play Peter? It's a fact." Mitch had probably read that long ago and filed it away until now. "Anyway, what are you gonna do? You're going back tomorrow?"

"Well, yeah. I wasn't sure for a while, but now I can't wait."

"You want me to come?"

"Well—maybe not. She might be upset if she's not expecting you. But I can maybe ask if she'll meet my friends."

Mitch got up to shoot a basket. "I'll wait by the front gate so you can tell me what happens."

"Yeah. As long as she shows up. I mean, I'm sure she'll show up."

Mitch shrugged. "Guess you'll find out."

Jessica's mother came home just before dark, looking about as tired as she usually did, and the two of them made dinner. Jessica told her about the girl she spoke to that morning (she didn't mention the really odd parts). Her mother said it was nice that Jessica was finally meeting some new people.

Chapter 2

The Summer Country

SLEEP DID NOT COME EASILY that night. Jessica flopped from side to side and plumped her pillow and even tried counting sheep for long minutes before she dropped off. In the early hours, she woke three different times and each time found it harder to fall back asleep. *I'm acting like a six-year-old at Christmas,* she thought, lying with her eyes closed in the dark.

Her mood did not improve at breakfast. She tried to act normally with her mother but couldn't make herself pay close attention to anything she said. Jessica picked at her cereal, gazed out the window, and left the house ten minutes early.

She walked past the bus stop without slowing her pace and then onto the bare path once the sidewalk ended. She veered into the dirt road without glancing to either side, and by the time she climbed the saddle between the hills and walked down into the hollow she had almost worn herself out from walking so fast.

But there was no need to hurry: the hollow seemed to be empty. She couldn't hear music or any other sound besides her own footsteps.

She found a flat rock near the road and sat on it. Maybe

she'd gotten there too soon; maybe all she had to do was wait. So she sat and waited, and nothing moved in the hollow except the shadows of a few crows.

After a long while she thought, *Five more minutes and that's it.* Twelve silent minutes later she knew she couldn't stay any longer. She stood up, brushing away some dirt and sighing an "Oh, well" that was supposed to sound mature and reasonable and only a little bit disappointed. Then she walked off down the road.

The first bell rang before the school was in sight. By the time Jessica reached the front gate the other students had already gone inside, all except Mitch. Jessica found him pacing impatiently under the steel arch. He jogged up to her as soon as he spotted her.

"Did you see her? What happened?" he said.

Jessica shrugged. "She didn't show."

"Oh." His shoulders sagged and he didn't bother trying to look mature or reasonable. "Shoot. That stinks."

"Yeah."

They walked through the gate and down the walkway to the quad, where their class schedules took them in different directions. Mitch said "Well, see you after school," and Jessica said "Okay." She wanted to say some other things—like *thanks*—but she didn't. And she got mad at herself for not saying them.

Today was Friday, the day when Jessica had the fewest number of classes. That was the good news. The bad news was that she had to attend the bi-monthly meeting of her Convergence Group. More than once she'd sensed a terrible injustice about holding the meetings on the last day of the week. On Mondays they would have been almost bearable, since you really couldn't make the day any worse.

At Esterhaus, which had grade levels from sixth up through high school, students from different grades rarely mingled. This looked natural enough to Jessica, but leaders at

18

Esterhaus seemed to treat the divisions as a defect (actually an *elevation opportunity*) and the Convergence Groups had been devised to address them. The student handbook described the groups as "a locus of mutual encouragement and support" where students could "break through artificial socio-economic barriers" and find "common ground in experiences of self-discovery." Jessica thought it likely that the person who wrote the handbook had never attended a group meeting.

This semester her group included four other people, all from higher grades. The oldest was Jackson Reese, a high school senior with a flair for dressing sharp; today he was wearing a linen sport coat over a crisp Tommy Hilfiger polo shirt and khaki slacks. The other boys were Rod Morales, who played on the school baseball team and seemed to prefer grunge-type outfits, and Huey Sanders, who was rather short, round, and curly-haired. They both walked into the room busily thumbing on their cell phones and continued without a break as they sat down.

The last member was Olivia LaRusso. Jessica had heard other girls speak of Olivia in tones bordering on reverence, regarding her as a fashion genius who could adopt nearly any style like a chameleon. At the last meeting she had been blonde and longhaired and dressed like a magazine model; today it appeared she'd gone Goth. Her dark skirt, top, and shawl had been carefully tailored to look handmade and her hair was now short, black, spiky, and streaked with colors. Two open bottles of nail polish sat on her desk, and while the others were arriving she carefully painted whorls of purple and black on her thumbnails.

Jessica, as usual, was wearing blue jeans and a shirt, and she'd never owned a cell phone since her mother couldn't afford the monthly bills. As luck would have it, today was her turn in the rotation to lead off the discussion. She cleared her throat and unfolded the paper that had been sent from the school office.

"Okay, umm . . . we can start, I guess. Here's the topic." She blinked at the sheet and read: "*We're in the last months of 1998, just over a year till the end of the millennium. It's like the threshold of a new age! Are we in the Esterhaus family doing all we can to prepare for the world that's coming? Group members should discuss how to manifest—*"

Without looking up from their activities most of the others groaned or made sounds of annoyance. "Not *again*," Olivia said. "Omigosh, aren't we done with that?"

"I want to know who writes the topics," Rod said, still keying on his phone.

"It's the seniors, like Jackson," Huey said. He'd brought out a deck of collectible game cards and began to sort them on his desk.

"And the counselors," Olivia said.

"But the seniors make the decisions," Huey said.

"That's right," Jackson said, pulling a stray thread off his jacket sleeve. "It takes some maturity. You aren't ready for it when you're a junior."

"You know what, Jackson?" Olivia said as she blew on her nails. "Last week I told my analyst about you, and she goes, 'Well, he must be some kind of *major* control freak.' You know, like you can't get involved in anything unless you're in charge."

Jackson snorted. "That's ridiculous. She shouldn't talk about someone she's never met. My analyst would *never* do that."

Jessica ventured to steer the discussion back on track. "Okay. But should we maybe talk about the topic, for a while? I mean it might be kind of...important...."

The others had all looked up, staring at Jessica as though shocked that any sort of sound could be coming from her general direction. She shrank back in her chair as far as physically possible.

"You know who *really* needs therapy?" Huey said. "Melissa Beals."

Jackson said, "Oh, what's up?" while Olivia sputtered a laugh. In confidential tones she said, "You know who she likes? You really wanna know? *Steve Mueller.*"

Rod laughed and pounded on his desk. Jackson said, "You've got to be kidding."

"I'm *serious*," Olivia said. "She comes up to me yesterday and goes, 'So Olivia, what do you think of Steve?' And I go, 'You mean Steve Drummond, with the blue Porsche?' And she goes 'No, no, no, Steve *Mueller.*' And all of a sudden I'm like ready to barf, okay? So I'm all 'Melissa, Steve Mueller is like the official junior class dweeb. I think he still lets his mother cut his hair.' And she goes 'Yeah, but don't you think he's kinda cute?' So I go...."

The meeting continued more or less in that manner until the lunch bell rang. Jessica made no other attempts to interrupt and no one bothered asking her any questions.

In the early afternoon she found herself walking in a hallway behind Olivia and another girl. The girl had been complaining that the Convergence Groups were a big waste of time, mostly because of the way they shoved so many different kinds of students together. Olivia laughed and said, "I know, right? I mean, the scrubs are just so *dumb*. They never have anything to say."

Jessica dug her fingernails into her palms and turned quickly into a side hallway where she could seethe in private. She half-expected to hear steam hissing out of her ears.

By the end of the day, if anything, her mood had sunk even further. She didn't want to see anyone or talk to anyone, she just wanted to go home and shut the door behind her. She avoided the front gate because she knew Mitch would be there and she didn't want to see him either. And mostly for the same reason—at least that's what she told herself—she decided to skip the bus and walk home.

She planned to stay close to the main road and ignore the shortcut. But the sun shone bright and hot that afternoon and every car that whipped by stirred up whirlwinds of dust. Before long her eyes smarted and her tongue tasted like a sandbox. When she came to the dirt road she veered into it without even thinking.

Whether or not she was ready to admit it, she really did want to visit the hollow again. She began looking and listening long before she came to the place she had met Ariel; but she could have saved herself the trouble. When the road finished its slow rise and leveled out in between the hills Jessica knew she was alone.

She stood in the middle of the road feeling hot and useless. A hawk soared on an updraft over one of the hills; she watched as it circled and banked, then decided to check the clearing one more time. After pushing through the dry thicket, a quick glance showed that the place was empty.

"It's not fair," she muttered, frowning at the bare ground. "It's really not fair." As she backed up towards the road and turned around, Ariel jumped in front of her and shouted *"Boo!"*

Jessica let out an *Aaaak!* and hopped back. Her foot slipped on a smooth rock and she sat down hard in the dirt with her arms flailing. Ariel shrieked with laughter and hopped from one leg to the other, pointing at Jessica and holding her sides.

Jessica glared. "That wasn't funny!"

"Yes it was! Yes it was!" Ariel said. "You should've seen your face! It was like...." She bugged out her eyes and dropped her jaw like a gasping fish.

"No, it wasn't! And where were you this morning? I waited and waited—" But Ariel wasn't listening. She'd begun dancing and playing a tune on her pipes, a melody that sounded suspiciously like *Jessica is a scaredy cat, Jessica is a scaredy cat.*

"Stop that, cut it out!" Jessica said, standing up.

Ariel broke off. "What do you mean?"

"You *know* what I mean. Stop making fun of me!"

"But I wasn't making fun of you," Ariel said.

"Oh yeah? When you jump up and scare me and then play that stupid song? Is that all you want, someone to make fun of?"

Jessica's anger had more to do with the frustrations she'd dealt with that day than anything Ariel had done. But it didn't help that Ariel looked so surprised and innocent, as though she really had no idea what Jessica was talking about. She watched Jessica with her head cocked to one side and then walked up and took her hand. "Okay, I got it. Jessica is a *serious* girl. A *very* serious girl. We can't be playing games when Jessica is here. Nope. We just have to sit down and be very, *very* serious."

Ariel sat in the road and tugged Jessica down so that the two of them faced each other. She put her elbows on her knees and her chin on her fists, then pressed her lips together and narrowed her eyes and wrinkled her forehead, making just about the most serious expression a person could make.

Don't laugh, Jessica thought, but she wasn't strong enough. Within five seconds her mouth began twitching, and moments later she and Ariel were both sputtering and giggling.

"So I looked silly, huh?" Jessica said.

"Yup. Silliest thing I ever saw."

Jessica mussed her hair with one hand. "Well, you look a whole lot funnier than me."

"Do not."

"Do so. So stop being mean. I go to all this trouble and you act like...but wait a minute, how do you pop out of nowhere like that? One minute I don't see you, then—"

Ariel jumped to her feet and pulled Jessica's arm. "Come on!" she said. "Come with me!"

"What? Where?" Jessica said, getting up. "I have to go home."

Ariel tugged her as she moved down the road. "To a special place. The Summer Country. And I'll get you home, I promise."

"What do you mean, the Summer...where is it?"

"First you have to shut your eyes."

"Right now? I'll fall on my face!"

"No you won't. Come on, please?" It seemed a very odd kind of game, but Ariel was clearly enjoying herself and Jessica hated to stop it. She closed her eyes, saying, "You'd better not let go!"

"I won't! Now when I make some music, you picture a green tree in your head and then jump, okay?"

Jessica laughed. "Are you doing another trick?"

"No, honestly. Get ready—one more second...."

Ariel blew a loud complicated chord; Jessica imagined a green tree and jumped. She felt slightly dizzy as she left the ground but she kept her feet under her and landed easily on firm earth. Beside her Ariel gave a squeal of delight, clapping her hands. Jessica said, "Can I look now?" and Ariel laughed and said, "Yes! Yes!"

Jessica opened her eyes. The road, the hollow, and the dried plants were all gone. She stood in a field of brilliant green grass, the blades almost reaching her knees. A gusting wind tossed her hair and spread ripples through the field. Far in the distance she could see folds and hills of the same rich green, broken here and there with strands of flowering trees, and over it all arched a sky so blue and deep that it made her eyes ache. She had never seen the place before, not even in her dreams.

Ariel ran up to her and threw her arms around her and said, "You did it! You did it! You did it!" She took her hands and danced around her, laughing and shouting, then broke away and did a cartwheel. Jessica watched her in a kind of daze; she caught her breath and said, "Ariel...Ariel...."

"What? What?" Ariel called, laughing again.

Jessica felt herself trembling and her voice rose. "What happened? Where is this?"

Ariel turned another cartwheel and landed, intentionally, flat on her back in the grass. "Look at me!" she called. "I can make a grass angel. Look!"

"Ariel, come *on*," Jessica said. "This isn't funny—"

Ariel hopped to her feet, her eyes sparkling. "Bet you can't catch me. Bet you can't!" She took off running across the field.

Jessica made an exasperated noise. "She can't sit still for one minute." The girl was already thirty yards away, running at the end of a long track through the grass. Jessica started after her, calling "Hey, wait up!"

Ariel twisted around, running backwards. "No! You have to catch me!"

"I don't *want* to catch you," Jessica called as she ran. "I want you to talk. Where did you take me?"

"I told you, it's the Summer Country. Isn't it great?"

"Sure. How do I get home?"

"You're such a worrywart! First I have to show you something. Follow me!" She turned and ran even faster.

Jessica kept up the chase. Little by little she realized that Ariel was right about one thing, at least: the place was certainly *great*. Once or twice in her life she had seen a sky as deep as that sky or hills as green as those hills, but never before had she tasted air so sweet and wild. It must have been carrying a hundred different scents, trees and earth and grasses and wildflowers, all of them so alive that Jessica wondered if anyone had ever smelled them before. She drew in a long breath and felt the blood rushing in her lungs. She laughed and spread out her arms and let the wind blow through her fingers, and her legs ran under her like they were never going to stop.

Jessica was a good runner but Ariel managed to stay out of reach. She led the way across acres of green fields and down a long angling slope with a stream at the bottom. They splashed through the stream, soaking Jessica's sneakers, and ducked into a grove of trees where the blossoms on the branches turned the air yellow and orange.

Ariel still wasn't done. Jessica followed her out of the grove and felt the ground rising. She looked up and saw they were climbing a tall hill, maybe the tallest she'd ever seen. She called out, "Where are you going? This is too high!"

"Wait till you see! It's wonderful!" Ariel called back, and kept on running.

Jessica toiled up after her. She gained on her as they neared the crest, and when the ground finally leveled out Ariel was only a few feet ahead. Before Jessica could speak Ariel took a running leap, shouting *"Wahooo,"* and dropped out of sight.

Jessica pulled up short. The other side of the hill fell away suddenly in front of her feet. It looked as steep as a breaking wave, even taller than the side they had come up. Far below she saw Ariel slipping and rolling, down and down through the fine grass like she was riding a snow slide.

Jessica's throat tightened, but she knew if she stopped to think it would be too late. She took a step back, shouted *"Cowabunga!"* and jumped off the edge.

It was the longest, softest, slipperiest, scariest slide anyone had ever taken. Jessica bounced and tumbled and slid, sometimes all at once, while blades of grass whipped and whistled past her ears. After a few blurred moments the slope began to ease, but Jessica still slid so fast that she wondered if she would stop before she hit something solid. But in the end the hill bottomed out easily in a meadow full of wildflowers. Jessica rolled to a stop only a yard or so from Ariel, who lay flat on her back breathless with laughter.

Jessica put her hands over her face and groaned. "Omigosh, omigosh," she said. "I don't *believe* I did that."

"Didn't I tell you?" Ariel said. "Wasn't it the best?"

"I thought I was gonna die."

"Oh, pooh. You really are a worrywart." She stretched her arms over her head as she said, "I love coming here. It's always like this, the wind and the sun and the grass. It's my absolutely favorite place anywhere."

Jessica flexed her arms and legs and fingers until she felt fairly certain no bones were broken. She rolled onto her stomach and watched Ariel, who had bent a stalk of tiny red blossoms down to her nose. Maybe the strangest thing about her, Jessica thought, was that she didn't seem strange. Her hair looked a mess and her cut-off jeans were kind of tattered, but for all that she could have passed for a kid in the neighborhood who'd been playing outside the whole day. None of this was making any sense.

"Okay, listen," Jessica said. "I caught you, right? So could we just stay here for a minute and would you *please* answer some questions?"

Ariel rolled her eyes. "How many? A whole bunch?"

"No, just a few, seriously." Now that she had the chance Jessica wasn't sure where to start. "So, umm...who *are* you? Or *what* are you?"

Ariel made a rude sound with her lips. "That's a dumb one. What do I look like?"

"Well—like a girl."

"There you go. What else?"

Jessica suspected she wouldn't get much further with that kind of question. She took a different tack. "This whole place," she said, waving around her, "the, uh, Summer Country. Where is this? I mean, are we somewhere on Earth?"

Ariel shook her head. "Nope. It's a different world."

Jessica tried to absorb the idea. "Umm...all right. Is this where you come from? Do you live here?"

Ariel looked surprised. "No, I just come here to play. I don't think anyone lives here. At least not yet." She started to say something else, then stopped and asked, "Hey, how about me? Can I ask a question? 'Cause I want to know, how does this place feel to you? Does it feel young?"

Jessica looked around. "Well...I didn't think about it, but yeah, you could say that. It kind of feels brand new."

Ariel nodded quickly. "Some places, you wouldn't believe how worn out they are. I get tired just being there. But this one, it's so young I think it's not even finished. Like maybe it's not ready for people yet." Ariel grinned. "Sometimes I think I'm not supposed to be here. I found it by accident and I never told anyone."

That raised even more questions. Before Jessica could ask them Ariel said, "Wait, I have another one. Did you know how to travel, before I met you?"

"What, you mean...travel to a place like this?"

"Uh-huh."

"Of course not."

"Well, that's funny," Ariel said, "because I knew you could do it. I could tell as soon as I met you."

"Huh? How?"

"You saw me. You heard my music."

Jessica stared at her. "So...I wasn't supposed to see you? Or hear you?"

"Nope."

"You mean you go around invisible all the time?"

"Pretty much. So I figured you could travel, too. I don't see why you hadn't found out—maybe it would happen when you were older. I'm not sure how it's supposed to work."

Jessica rested her chin on one fist and frowned at the ground. "This just keeps getting weirder," she muttered. When she looked up Ariel was standing and brushing off the front of her shirt. "I promised you wouldn't get home late," she said. "It's probably time to go, huh?"

Jessica sighed. "Yeah. If I'm not waiting for my mom, she always thinks I've been kidnapped."

Ariel played a short tune on her pipes (she had a cord slung crosswise over a shoulder, and Jessica noticed she hung the instrument there when she wasn't using it). She frowned as she stopped. "It's trickier going back. You'll have to stand a special way, like this."

Ariel put her left hand on one knee and made a fist with her right hand; Jessica, hesitating, managed to copy her. "And you have to have a different picture in your head," Ariel said. "It's like, umm...a blue walrus."

Jessica laughed. "A walrus?"

"Well, sort of like that, and it has to be bright blue. And don't forget the whiskers."

"So...I just have to think about it?"

"Yeah. Make the picture."

Jessica closed her eyes and made the picture. Ariel played a long single tone that seemed to vibrate through Jessica's body like she was a tuning fork. Then Ariel pushed on her shoulders—

—and she fell backwards a long, long way, much longer than it should have taken to hit the ground. She felt herself gliding, drifting like a falling leaf—

—until she stopped with a *thump*. She blinked and saw a familiar-looking tree; it was the oak tree behind the bus stop near her home. Across the road the school bus from Esterhaus was sliding to a stop with a squeal of brakes. The air felt hot and stuffy, like most afternoons that time of year.

Jessica got to her feet just as Ariel rushed up to hug her. "That was the most fun *ever*," she said. "I want to see you again, okay? Can I come back in a few days? I won't play any more tricks, I promise."

"Uh, sure. That would be great," Jessica managed to say.

29

"Okay! Bye! See you soon!" She vanished with a *whuff* like a blown-out candle.

Jessica took a long breath and rubbed her hip; before she could do anything else Ariel was back. "You go to school, right?" she said. "You go to that place over the hill, with all the people who dress funny?"

"Yeah. That sounds like Esterhaus."

"Can I come see you there?"

"Well...sure. Why not?"

"Okay! Bye now!" Ariel gave her another hug and vanished again.

Jessica hardly had time to move before she heard crunching footfalls in the dry oak leaves. "Hey Jessie!" came Mitch's voice behind her. "You're home already? I figured you were walking again. Did you get a ride? And how come you were talking just now?" Before she could respond he looked down and said, "Hey, your shoes are soaked. How'd that happen?"

Jessica stared at her feet. "I—I was...." There didn't seem any way to start. She wrinkled her nose and said, "You are really, *really* not going to believe this."

She began the story while they walked down the sidewalk towards her home. Inside in the kitchen she got out a carton of milk and some chocolate chip cookies, and Mitch worked his way through four of them in the time it took her to finish.

"So, when you came up to me under the tree," she said, "you didn't see Ariel, right? I was the only one there?"

Mitch finished a drink of milk and gave a long burp. "Excuse me. Yup, just you."

"Okay, so that part was true too. And maybe that's the craziest thing." She looked at Mitch as he chose another cookie. "Hey, you believe me, don't you?"

"Well, yeah," Mitch said, surprised. "I mean, I'm trying. It's just...it's like...I don't know, the weirdest thing I ever heard. It's not a cartoon anymore, it's the Twilight Zone."

"I know." Jessica leaned her face on a fist. "I'm not afraid of her, you know. Most of the time she acts like a normal kid. But even *that* doesn't make any sense." After a moment she muttered, "I hate it when I don't know what's going on. That's when bad things happen."

Mitch said, "You gonna tell your Mom?"

"No. Or I don't think so. She wouldn't get it, and she already worries about me too much. But I wish there was somebody who could figure this out."

"Yeah." Mitch stopped before he could take another bite. "Hey, you know who you could talk to?"

"Who?"

"Mr. McNulty."

"What, the history teacher?"

"Yeah."

"Come on."

"No, really. He knows all kinds of stuff. And he's a great guy. Did I tell you about how he tutored me after my operation?" Mitch had been born with his right leg a couple inches shorter than his left, and earlier that year he'd gone through an operation to correct it. When he wore shorts last summer Jessica had seen the long thick scar, running down the back of his leg like a highway on a map. "It was his idea. I used to go to his house all the time. You wouldn't believe the library he's got, all these books in Latin and German, and he reads them like they were English."

"Well, good. And I liked his class. But...." She made a sour face. "He's a *teacher*, you know. I couldn't talk to someone like that, I'd feel like a little kid telling stories."

"You wouldn't if you saw—" Mitch froze with the glass halfway to his mouth. Jessica waited, then said, "Saw? Saw what?"

Mitch put the glass down. "Nothing."

"What do you mean, nothing? What are you talking about?"

Mitch chewed his lip, looking as though he wanted to talk, but he shook his head and said, "I can't tell you."

"Why not?"

"I can't tell you that either."

Jessica pounded on the table. "Mitch Carlucci, don't you *do* this. Don't start keeping secrets on me!"

"But...okay, listen. We could go tomorrow, to Mr. McNulty's house. It's only a couple miles. And we could, umm—see what happens." Jessica was still fuming. "Look, it's not a big deal. I mean it's even kind of silly. But if he, uhh...if he does what I think he'll do then maybe you'll talk to him. Okay?"

Jessica kept glaring but didn't feel like fighting any longer. "Fine, we can go. But if you're trying to pull something on me you're in *big* trouble."

"Oh, right. Now I'm *really* scared," Mitch said. He ducked out the door before Jessica could throw a cookie.

Chapter 3

Mr. McNulty's Secret

SATURDAY DAWNED as an excellent day for a bike ride: the weather had cooled overnight and a smooth layer of clouds blanketed the sun. Jessica was already waiting at the curb when Mitch rode up on his mountain bike, a gift from his grandparents after his operation; it boasted a complex assemblage of gears, levers, cables, and knobs.

"All set?" he said, squeezing a handbrake as he pedaled backwards.

"Yeah," Jessica said. "But, umm...."

"What?"

She shook her head. "You're *sure* this is a good idea?"

"Totally. It'll be great, you'll see."

Jessica climbed onto her own bicycle—an older bike with no gears, and almost too small for her now, but still (she felt certain) the fastest bike in the neighborhood—and followed Mitch around the curve at the bottom of the street and out to the main road. They crossed over when the traffic was clear and rode along the shoulder, heading up the valley.

The road skirted the feet of a few hills and dived in and out of the shade of some dark oak trees. Jessica fell back a few yards behind Mitch and muttered under the road noise: "This won't work. I just know it."

Mitch couldn't seem to grasp the kinds of problems Jessica faced in talking with adults, men in particular. Things only got worse when the adult had some kind of authority, like a police officer or—maybe worst of all—a schoolteacher. Just now the thought of telling Mr. McNulty about Ariel made Jessica's hands clammy. She could picture herself tongue-tied and stuttering, mixing up words and waving her hands to fill in the blanks. He would snort or laugh or look at her with that smug look grownups get when a kid is telling an obvious lie.

I would die right there, she thought. *I would crawl under a rock and no one would find me ever again.*

But she'd never found a way to explain this to Mitch, who had an amazing knack for talking to anyone, anywhere, as though it were the simplest thing in the world. Jessica had marveled at his abilities and tried to puzzle them out, but without success. She only knew that if she tried to describe her fears he would call her "nutcase" or "fruit loops" or dismiss it as some kind of girl thing.

So she felt stuck. "Maybe it'll be fine, maybe I really am a worrywart," she muttered. But as she rode along the rhythm of the bike seemed to be saying: *...BAD-idea...BAD-idea...BAD-idea....*

They passed a small shopping center and part of a new housing tract, where most of the lots were newly graded and only a few had concrete slabs. Not long after that Mitch turned left into a smaller side street. The road narrowed quickly and the asphalt gave way to gravel that crunched under their tires. They began to see older-looking houses along either side, some with split-log fences and gates, and many of the yards had one or two enormous trees. The street was quiet, even on a Saturday morning, and Jessica had a feeling that very few kids lived in that neighborhood.

Mitch angled his bike across the road and braked beside a mailbox at the edge of a small lawn. Below the mailbox hung a weathered plaque with "McNULTY" carved in large letters. The house that sprawled around the lawn looked large and awkward; it was painted mustard yellow with a wood-shingled roof, and beyond the roofline Jessica could see the tops of nearby hills.

Mitch said, "Shoot, the cars are gone. I don't think they're home. That was dumb, I should've called first."

"Seriously?" Jessica said. She could feel the tension draining from her shoulders. "Well, no problem. We can just go home."

"There's no rush. Maybe they just went to the store."

"No, we should go." She tightened her hands on the handlebars. "Mitch—it's good I don't have to do this. I know it sounds stupid but I don't want to talk to a grownup about this stuff. Really. I don't think I could say it right. It's better if we just go home. Is that okay?"

"Well—yeah, sure," he said, looking surprised.

"I should've told you sooner—"

"Nah, no big deal. I didn't want to *make* you do anything, you know—"

"I know. Sorry for being a pain—"

"Nah. It's fine, we'll go. I'll see him another day."

She felt grateful he was making it easy. He turned his bike and put a foot on a pedal, but before he could push off, a car rushed past them and turned sharply into the McNultys' driveway. It was an old-style Volkswagen beetle, bright yellow between the rust spots, and it gave a friendly *beep beep* as the engine wheezed off.

A woman stepped out of the driver's side and called, "Hello, Mitch, good to see you! Didn't know you were coming." She looked slender and older, with salt-and-pepper hair tied in a knot behind her head.

"Yeah, it's kind of a surprise," Mitch said. "I brought my friend Jessica today. Jessie, this is Mrs. McNulty. Her name's Katherine but she tells everyone to call her Katie."

"Pleased to meet you, Jessica," Katie said, shaking her hand. She had a strong grip and her eyes were almost piercingly bright. "I haven't met many of Mitch's friends. If you've come to see George, though, you're fresh out of luck. He went out earlier and I've no idea when he'll be back."

"Yeah, I figured," Mitch said. "No problem."

Jessica added, "We were just going to head home—"

"Well, now, don't you be like that," Katie said. "You can't ride so far on a warm day and turn around empty-handed. You come inside now and have some iced tea before you go." She walked up the lawn as though the matter was settled.

Mitch looked at Jessica; she twisted her face and shrugged as though to say, *Do we have a choice?* They left their bikes at the curb and followed Katie.

Inside the house they entered a darkened living room that smelled of wood polish and pipe tobacco. Comfortable-looking furniture had been stationed around a coffee table, with patterns on the fabrics that looked like old-style book illustrations. Katie said, "I won't be a minute," and went off to the kitchen. Mitch sat on the sofa and Jessica joined him, perching on the edge.

"One glass, then we go?" she said in a low voice, and Mitch nodded.

Even in her awkwardness Jessica felt curious—particularly about Katie, who seemed an odd match for Mr. McNulty. When she returned with the iced tea Jessica saw that she wore tooled leather boots under a long denim skirt, and over her blouse hung a necklace made of silver and polished stones. While she was in the kitchen she had stuck two ivory-colored chopsticks through her thick knot of hair.

"Sorry the timing's bad, Jessica, but it was good of you to

come," Katie said, pouring a glass. "Were you one of George's students?"

"Yes, ma'am—Katie," she said.

"Jessie was in European History," Mitch said.

"Uh-huh. I enjoyed it. I was sorry when Mr. McNulty left."

"Well, he was sorry too, though he'd never say so, after the way they treated him," she said with a sharp look. "That was a shameful episode, if you ask me."

"Yeah, the whole thing stunk," Mitch said.

"And I know George misses the teaching, though he'd never admit that either." She leaned closer to Jessica with a confiding look. "He's no good at being retired, you know. Absolutely *terrible* at it and always getting underfoot. I'm not a violent person, understand, but I believe I could do some serious damage if he doesn't find something to do, *very* soon."

Jessica figured that Katie was mostly joking but she had no idea how to respond. Before she could make an attempt, the front door rattled. Katie brightened and said, "Oh, you're in luck. There's George now."

Jessica snapped her head towards the door. It rattled again and swung open on complaining hinges, and Mr. McNulty slouched through, looking larger than he had at Esterhaus, almost bumping the frame with his shoulders and his balding head. He blinked through thick glasses, grumbling under his breath, and Jessica felt her stomach twist as though someone had pulled it into a knot.

"George, just in time," Katie said. "Mitch dropped by, and he brought a friend."

"What? Young Mitchell, is it?" Mr. McNulty said, his face twitching as though fighting off a sneeze. "Hmff. Didn't know you were coming."

"We've been having some tea," Katie said. "Come and sit. Oh, actually you can take my glass, come to think of it." She put a hand on Jessica's arm. "Jessica, I apologize, I need to rush off, there are calls I have to make before lunch. But I'm glad to have met you, please come back when I can visit longer." Jessica wanted to say *No, don't go*, but couldn't get her mouth working before Katie left the room.

Mr. McNulty walked closer with a heavy tread. "So who's this then? Ahh—the Blackwater girl? From European History?"

"Yes, sir," Mitch said. "Jessica. From last semester."

"Last semester. Hmm. I've had better classes than that one. Some that were worse." He took hold of an armchair, dragging it with loud scraping sounds, and when it bumped the coffee table Jessica almost jumped. He lowered himself into the seat with another *hmff* and turned to Jessica, large enough to loom over her, his eyes owlish behind the lenses.

"So. To what do I owe the pleasure?" he said.

Jessica swallowed. "Umm..." she said.

"Not a social call, I suppose. Not many students drop in out of the blue. I see Mitch often enough but that's about it. So is there something we should talk about?"

"Umm," Jessica said again, and stopped dead.

It was happening exactly as she'd feared, or even worse. Her throat had clamped shut and her brain was seizing like an engine with sand in the gears. Any moment now she would start stuttering and making silly gestures with her hands. She turned to Mitch with a pleading look: *Say something, please!* He seemed to understand, at least in part, because he straightened and spoke quickly.

"Well, sir, this wasn't Jessie's idea, really—I wanted to come today and I invited her along. We've been friends a long time so I hope it's okay...."

"O'course," Mr. McNulty shrugged. "No need to ask."

"Good," Mitch said, and Jessica managed to breathe out. He continued, "But you know, there *was* something we wanted to tell you today—" Jessica gritted her teeth, trying to shake her head with tiny movements. "—and it was my idea to talk to you, but it's something that happened to Jessie...."

No, no, stop right there—

"...something really strange that she can't figure out. You're the only one I knew who could maybe make sense of it—"

Don't, please don't—

"—especially if you could hear the story from her like I did—"

No, no, no, no—

"—but it's tough to describe. And I was thinking it might help, it could help a lot, if you would show her Sidewinder Gap."

Silence fell after he spoke. Jessica blinked: *What was he talking about?* She turned and saw that Mr. McNulty had gone shockingly still, his eyes narrowed and his hands flat on his knees. He spoke in a low voice. "Young man, that information is privileged."

"I know, sir."

"It was not to be shared. Did you forget that?"

"No, sir," Mitch said, still unruffled. "Jessie knows nothing except the name, and she only heard it just now. If you want, we'll leave now and that'll be the end of it. But I hope—I hope you know that I wouldn't have gone this far unless it was very important."

Mr. McNulty went silent again. He smoothed his hair with one hand, then took off his glasses and cleaned the lenses with a handkerchief. He put the glasses back on and leaned forward on his elbows, cracking the knuckles of one hand against his other palm.

"Lots of reasons to say no. You know that," he said. "So I won't bother arguing. And you know I have some confidence in your judgment. So, here's the question: do you believe, as far as you can figure it, that this is truly the best thing to do?"

"Yes, sir," Mitch said. "But it's completely your choice."

Mr. McNulty frowned but didn't speak. He seemed to consider something, then thought better of it, then shook his head. With an audible huff he stood from the chair, muttering "*Might as well put up a billboard*," and walked out of the room towards the kitchen. Mitch whispered to Jessica, "Let's go," and they got up to follow.

They hurried through the kitchen and into the pantry, where Mr. McNulty was opening the back door of the house. He left it open as he stepped outside but didn't look back.

They followed him off the porch and onto a path that passed through a kitchen garden, with vegetables planted in well-tended rows and herbs growing in raised circles. At the bottom of the garden the walkway crossed a line of citrus trees. Mr. McNulty pushed aside some branches that hung over the path, and when they swung back Mitch and Jessica had to duck to avoid the lemons.

Beyond the trees they entered a wide fenced yard not far from the base of the hills. Ahead of them stood a building that looked like a small cottage or a very large shed. Some sections of the walls and roof met at awkward angles, as though the building had been enlarged a few times without giving much thought to appearances. The path led to a door at the corner of the shed; Mr. McNulty strode up to it and unlocked it with a key from his pocket. Mitch followed him inside and Jessica came after, stepping carefully.

They had entered a small room, almost too small for the three of them. Set against the right-hand wall was a bookshelf that held nothing but a single battered metal box. Opposite the shelves was a closed door with several electrical switches mounted beside it, some of them rather large and marked with CAUTION signs.

Mr. McNulty flipped a switch and the overhead light came on; he flipped another and Jessica saw light leaking under the closed door. Then he worked through the remaining switches one by one. Jessica began to hear humming sounds that grew louder as Mr. McNulty finished the last large switch.

He turned to the shelves and put his hand on the metal box. "Jessica," he said. "I've seen that you're serious about responsibilities—you proved that in class. That makes this easier for me."

"Oh," Jessica said. "Umm...thanks."

"I want you to know, I'm about to trust you in a way that I've trusted very few people. I hope you appreciate that. More than that, I hope you're going to respect it."

"Yes, sir," she said, squeezing her fists as she found her voice again. "I will. You can count on me."

"I'm sure that's true." He opened the battered metal box, then reached inside and pulled out three folded hats. They had bills on the front like baseball caps but they were made of some type of cloth, with narrow blue and white stripes.

He opened a cap and placed it on Jessica's head. "Dispatcher," he said.

He opened the second and placed it on Mitch. "Conductor."

He placed the last one on his own head and straightened the bill. "Chief engineer." Then he gestured to the inner door, saying, "Lead the way, Mitch."

Mitch opened the door and stepped through with Jessica behind him, and as she entered the room she said "Omigosh" and stopped still.

The inside of the building looked larger, almost, than the outside, as big as two or three garages joined together. From end to end and wall to wall the space was filled with a landscape from a miniature world. Jessica saw a mountain range with waterfalls, tunnels, rocky crags, and high summits surrounded by storm clouds; rolling hills and thick forests, and rivers rushing through canyons into blue lakes with sailboats on the water; farms with crops planted in careful rows and cows grazing in the meadows; towns with storefront shops, movie theaters, and trolley cars;

railway stations with roundhouses, water towers, and figures waiting on the platforms. Through it all wound shining strands of train tracks, swooping and crossing at four or five different levels.

Jessica blinked and everything shifted. She saw that the storm clouds were cotton gauze, the lakes were made of blue glass, and the animals, trees, and buildings had been constructed out of wood or metal, carefully painted with endless details. Then she noticed the trains waiting on the tracks and she understood what she was seeing. "It's a train set," she said.

"Yeah, isn't it incredible?" Mitch said. "He calls it 'Sidewinder Gap.' He made the whole thing himself. Took him twenty-five years."

"So far," Mr. McNulty said.

Jessica looked around the room. "But it's a train set," she said.

"Not *just* a train set," Mitch said. "Look at that mountain range! And it's got five different towns. He built everything from scratch, except the engines. It's the coolest thing I've ever seen."

Jessica looked at both of them. "But that's what this was all about? A *train set?*"

Mitch made a pinched face and turned to Mr. McNulty. "Maybe it's a guy thing," he said.

Mr. McNulty shrugged. "I could've warned you."

"I mean, you're right, it looks awesome," Jessica said. "It's all amazing. But it's, umm...well, why make it a big secret? Lots of people would love to see this, I bet."

"That's the problem," Mitch said. "He doesn't want the attention, he thinks it would ruin it."

Mr. McNulty snorted. "I've seen it happen. A guy builds a decent layout, shows it to the neighbors. People start dropping by out of the blue just to have a look. Before you know it, school buses are pulling up for field trips. So you either keep it quiet or you've got a tourist attraction. I know a few other modelers and we get together now and again and have some fun. That's plenty for me."

"Okay. It makes sense," Jessica said. "And I promise I'll never talk about it. But...the trains work, right? You can run them and everything?"

Mitch grinned and tugged on his cap. "That's what we're here for, ma'am."

Getting started was more difficult than Jessica expected. The controls had been built into the middle of the layout and reaching them required squeezing behind a shelf that supported the mountain range. Once the three of them were settled Mitch showed Jessica how to operate the switches and throttles, and very quickly all four trains were running smoothly on the tracks.

Over the rattling of the cars Mr. McNulty explained the background of the layout: he had names for all the geographic features and histories for each of the towns. Even the engines had stories, down to the years they'd been built and the names of their engineers. Jessica felt certain that her locomotive, a classic steam engine, was the best of the four. Small puffs of steam rose from the smokestack as it ran along and the passenger cars were lit from the inside, showing silhouettes of people in the windows. She found it easy to imagine that the train moved through a world full of people and families that took trips to new places, or sometimes just stayed at home and hardly ever fought with each other.

Sometime later Mr. McNulty said, "Don't know about you two, but I'm ready for lunch." On the wall clock Jessica saw that two hours had passed; it had felt more like thirty minutes. They brought the engines back to the stations and slid out of the layout.

On the path back to the house Mitch and Jessica dropped

behind Mr. McNulty. Mitch said quietly, "Cool, huh? He's a great guy, like I said."

"Yeah. Who knew?"

"So, you want to talk to him?"

"Umm...we'll see."

From the refrigerator in the kitchen Mr. McNulty pulled out cheeses and lunchmeats and jars of mustard and mayonnaise while Mitch retrieved the sliced bread and pickles. In short order they were assembling large sandwiches at the kitchen table. As they worked Mitch told Jessica about Mr. McNulty's next project, an all-wooden trestle over a mountain gorge. "He said I could do some of the construction. You want to help?"

"Sure, if it's okay," Jessica said. Then to Mr. McNulty: "You know, sir...I know I made things awkward when we came here today. It wasn't fair to put you on the spot—"

Mr. McNulty shook his head. "Don't give it a thought. Katie says I'm gettin' grumpy in my old age, and she might be right. Just glad you had a good time."

"Yeah, I did. Thanks for trusting me." Then without giving herself time to think: "And if it's all right, I'd like to trust *you* with something."

Between bites of her sandwich Jessica told him the whole tale (with only an occasional stutter), from the time she first heard the music outside the hollow to the moment Ariel disappeared after bringing her home from the Summer Country. Mr. McNulty listened without asking questions, nodding now and then and tapping a finger on his chin when he wasn't eating.

When Jessica finished he looked thoughtful but didn't speak. Mitch said, "So, whaddya think?"

"*Wellllll...*" he drawled, "this is either the most interesting thing I've ever heard or the nuttiest. Hard to say which."

"Just so you know, Jessie would never make this up—"

Mr. McNulty waved him off. "She's not lying, and neither are you. So something else is going on. But, you know, invisible people, jumping to other places...." He shook his head. "I can't make heads or tails of it. Don't see how it fits."

Jessica nodded and said, "I feel the same way." But when she turned to Mitch, she was almost startled to find him grinning like a cat.

"Sir, if you ask me," Mitch said, "I'd say this calls for a *research* project."

Mr. McNulty looked at him over the top of his glasses. "You serious about that, young man?"

"Very serious."

"You talking about *genuine* research, or that spineless, weak-kneed, two-bit, academic type?"

"*Genuine* research," Mitch said. This was beginning to sound like a standard routine between the two of them.

"No holds barred?"

"No holds barred."

"Starting now, or sometime later when it's convenient?"

"Starting right now," Mitch said as his grin widened. "To the books, sir?"

"Indeed. To the books, young Mitchell, and be quick about it!"

Mitch hopped up from the table and ran out of the kitchen with Mr. McNulty close behind. Jessica managed to keep up as they crossed the living room into a hallway that led to the back of the house.

At the end of the hall they stepped into an airy, high-ceilinged room that looked very much like a library. Most of the space had been packed with books, from the well-ordered shelves that lined the walls to the overflowing bookcases in the middle of the room, not to mention the piles and stacks that took up the better part of the floor. An antique blackboard hung on one wall, with a nearby table serving as the only furniture.

With hardly a word Mitch and Mr. McNulty darted from

place to place, grabbing books and stacking them on the table. They brought dictionaries in two or three languages, thesauruses, books of mythology, histories, atlases, collections of classical literature, and some large old volumes Jessica didn't recognize. Within a few minutes the entire tabletop had been loaded two or three books deep. Mitch dropped a last volume on the pile and said, "All present and accounted for, sir."

Mr. McNulty took a piece of chalk and began rolling it between his palms, just as he had often done in class. "All right then," he said, "the only way to start this kind of thing is to ask good questions. Otherwise you waste a lot of time spinning your wheels. So think about that. What's the first question we want to ask?"

Mitch stuck his hand in the air, and Jessica laughed. "We're not in school, dummy. Just say it."

"Okay, fine. The first thing I want to know is, who is Ariel?" Mr. McNulty wrote on the chalkboard: WHO (OR WHAT) IS ARIEL? "Let's frame the questions as broad as possible and see where they take us," he said.

"Maybe we could start with her name, 'cause it's unusual," Mitch said. "I think the only place I've seen it is in that Disney movie about the little mermaid."

"Yeah, but that's no help," Jessica said.

"Even so, the name might take us somewhere," Mr. McNulty said. "Let's follow it out." He handed Mitch a copy of *Bullfinch's Mythology* and gave Jessica *The Golden Bough*. "Go for the indexes. I'll check the Oxford Classical Dictionary."

Mitch flipped through the pages at the back of the book, then shook his head. "No 'Ariels' in Bullfinch's. I guess that means she doesn't show up in Greek or Roman mythology. Too bad."

Jessica found the right page in her own index, but the name wasn't there. "Nothing here either," she said.

Mr. McNulty snapped his book closed. "Ditto for the OCD. So much for the classical period. Where to next?"

"How about regular dictionaries?" Mitch said. They each grabbed one and dug in. After some page flipping Mitch said, "I've got something, sort of. *Ariel: a gazelle native to Western Asia and Africa.* Never heard of that before."

"Here's another," Jessica said. "*In the book of Isaiah, an appellation applied to Jerusalem.* What's an 'appellation'?"

"It's like a nickname, I think," Mitch said.

"That's about right," Mr. McNulty said. "Isaiah must have used the word 'Ariel' to refer to Jerusalem. But it doesn't tell us why he did it, unfortunately."

"I've got more," Mitch said. "*In the poetry of John Milton, the name of an angel.* You know, I thought about that already, could she be a kind of angel? She sounds like it sometimes in your stories."

"Well...I've never felt she talks or acts like an angel," Jessica said. "Not like I know much about it. Maybe we could find out how they act in John Milton's books." She looked in her own dictionary and said, "I've got another one too. *A character in Shakespeare's play The Tempest, described as 'an airy spirit.'*"

"Ah, now this could get interesting," Mr. McNulty said, as though he'd been expecting it. He dug out *The Complete Works of William Shakespeare* and leafed through it. "Haven't seen 'The Tempest' in a while but I remember the character. Shakespeare wrote it as a male character, actually. He's a magical creature who plays music on a flute. What's more, there are only a few people who can see him and talk to him. Here we are—this is Prospero the sorcerer, talking to Ariel:

> *Go, make thyself like to a nymph of the sea;*
> *Be subject to no sight but mine; invisible*
> *To every eye-ball else.*

"Wow, that's pretty close," Mitch said.

"But 'The Tempest' wasn't a true story, was it?" Jessica said.

"Nope," Mr. McNulty said. "Shakespeare made up the whole thing, as far as anyone knows."

"That's what I thought. So is this telling us anything important?"

"Too early to say. The first rule of research: don't throw anything away. You never know when the connections are going to happen." He turned to the blackboard and made some notes:

```
GAZELLE
ISAIAH/JERUSALEM
MILTON/ANGEL
SHAKESPEARE/THE AIRY SPIRIT
```

They looked at the blackboard for a while. Mitch said, "Maybe Jessica's right: I don't know if we're getting very far."

"In that case, let's ask another question," Mr. McNulty said.

"Okay, how's this," Jessica said. "When I traveled with Ariel we went to another world—at least that's what she said. But is that possible? Like, scientifically?"

"Let's take that in two steps," Mr. McNulty said. On the blackboard he wrote: 1. ARE THERE OTHER WORLDS? "We already have an answer for that one." He wrote YES, MOST LIKELY and underlined it.

"Seriously?" Jessica said. "Are you talking about planets?"

"Other planets, and more than that. You've heard of 'cosmology,' I expect? People trying to figure out how the universe works. I've read books by cosmologists, so I've learned just enough to be dangerous. But some have been saying that if you could see the whole thing, you might see a whole bunch of universes all fitted inside each other, like layers of an onion. Or like one of those Russian dolls: open it up and there's another doll, open that one and there's another, and on and on."

"Yeah, I've heard about that," Mitch said. "Has anybody proved it? Like, can we see those other worlds, if they're there?"

"Nope, can't be done, supposedly. We can't see out and those other places can't see in. But they could practically be beside us, even so."

"Weird," Jessica said. She tried to imagine herself at home or at school with another world somewhere around every corner, close enough to touch. The idea felt a little too crazy and she shook her head. "Do people—cosmologists—really think that?"

"Seems like some take it very seriously."

"Then how would you get from one world to another?"

Mr. McNulty wrote on the board: 2. CAN WE TRAVEL TO THEM? "That's the tough part," he said. "Those same people say we're pretty much stuck where we are. They figure if energy can't pass from one universe to another, there's no way for humans to do it."

"That's what I was afraid of," Jessica said.

"Yeah...but there's something else..." Mitch said. He had turned to look down and away, his forehead wrinkling as though he was chasing an idea. "I was thinking about all the stories you hear about traveling to other worlds. Like fairy tales about underground kingdoms. Or in the *Odyssey*, all those weird places with monsters."

"Yeah, or *Gulliver's Travels*," said Jessica. "And *The Wizard of Oz*."

"Right—so you wonder where that idea came from. Maybe once in a while people traveled like that and came back to tell about it. But the traveling would have to be tricky, or, umm—or else lots of people would do it."

"So, what? You're thinking it's magic?" Jessica said.

49

"Uh...no," Mitch said. His gaze was still vague, locked on something outside the room. "Maybe numbers."

Jessica wrinkled her nose. "Numbers?"

"Yeah. Or resonances. Or harmonics. But it's simpler to focus on numbers." He blinked at Jessica, his blue eye unusually bright. "I got to wondering, what if it's sort of like a formula? Like if you arrange the different pieces or values or whatever—in the right way, at the right time—you could connect to another world."

Jessica wasn't following this very well but Mr. McNulty wrote on the board, NUMBERS = FORMULA = CONNECTION??? "Interesting," he said. "Not sure where you got this, but it's not totally crazy."

"It's not?" Jessica said.

"Well, hear me out. There's a strange connection between mathematics and the real world. I'm out of my league here—again—but the fact is, everything's somehow organized or ordered around numbers and formulas. Nobody understands it but everyone kind of accepts it. Sunlight or galaxies or atomic particles, it's all the same: when people learn something new about the universe they use mathematics to describe it. So if there were a way to jump to another world—*if*, I'm saying—you'd expect that numbers would be built into it, somehow. That's all."

"All right...I guess," Jessica said. "But what does that have to do with Ariel?"

"Okay, listen," Mitch said. "When you came back from the Summer Country, Ariel played some music, right? And you had to think about a blue walrus."

"Right. And it still seems ridiculous."

"Yeah. But I started thinking: what does all that have in common? So first the music. People are always saying how music is mathematical—the sounds and rhythms and how they all fit together. Like every piece follows a kind of formula."

"Okay," Jessica said. It never surprised her anymore when Mitch got going like this. She also knew that by the time he was done it would probably make some kind of sense.

"And there's the color blue," Mitch said. "Colors are frequencies of light. And a frequency is a vibration—"

"—and it's measured with numbers," Jessica said.

"Right."

"Okay, Mr. Wizard, so what about the walrus?"

"Yeah, I didn't know what to do about that. But just now I thought: didn't Ariel say the picture should be 'sort of like' a walrus?"

"Yeah."

"So, what if the walrus wasn't the point? What if the important thing was the shape?"

"Ah-hah!" Mr. McNulty said. "Now I see it, young Mitchell. Excellent, just excellent!"

Jessica looked at both of them. "Okay, call me dumb, but I don't get it."

Mitch said, "One thing Mr. McNulty taught me is there's a type of mathematics that's about shapes. It's called Topology." Mr. McNulty was already writing things on the chalkboard: MUSIC, COLOR, SHAPE. "They use it for lots of stuff, astronomy and architecture and 3D computer programs. If you look at it that way, every shape, even if it's in your head, gives you a whole bunch of numbers, a really big calculation."

When Mr. McNulty finished his writing, it looked like this:

```
MUSIC => FORMULA
COLOR => FREQUENCY
SHAPE => TOPOLOGY
= CALCULATIONS = CONNECTIONS???
```

"All right," Jessica said. "You mean that when you bring those things together, it's like making a formula in your head."

"Yeah," Mitch said. "And if you do it right—if you kind of 'solve' it...."

"You go *poof*," Jessica said. "And you're somewhere else."

"Right."

Jessica chewed her lip, thinking about it. "I don't know, doesn't it sound too simple? If it's just about numbers why haven't people figured it out before?"

"Maybe some people have, like we were saying," Mitch said. "Maybe you have to get it just right and it's not easy."

"Or maybe there's more to it and we don't know what it is," Jessica said.

"Right."

They stared at the chalkboard in silence. Mr. McNulty said, "A lot of questions and not many answers."

"Yeah, but at least the questions look pretty good," Mitch said.

"So does this mean we're stuck already?" Jessica said.

"What do you say, Mitch?" Mr. McNulty said. "What do you do when the research hits a wall? Throw in the towel and call it quits?"

"No sir," he said. "You go back to the source and make more observations."

"Exactly right. Jessica, I believe your friend told you she was planning to see you again in a few days. Do you suppose the young lady would answer a few questions?"

"She might, if I can get her to hold still."

"Then how about we put our heads together and decide what to ask?"

They spent the rest of the afternoon working on the questions. All in all, Jessica thought later, it was one of the best days she'd had in a very long time.

Chapter 4

The Hidden Keys

JESSICA KEPT a careful watch for Ariel over the next several days. The girl had said she would come find her at Esterhaus, and Jessica realized it would probably be pointless to look for her anywhere else. Going back to the hollow, for example, would certainly be a complete waste of time.

She went anyway, on three different days, in the morning and afternoon. Each time she found the place empty and each time she felt disappointed, and then felt annoyed with herself for getting her hopes up.

At school she kept alert as she walked between classes or sat with other kids in the lunch area. An image repeatedly popped up in her head, a picture of Ariel wandering from place to place on the campus, puzzling at the unfamiliar faces and giving up in frustration. It seemed a silly idea (another one), but Jessica couldn't help looking for her every time she turned a corner in the hallways.

Only at home at the end of the day did she let her guard down. One evening after about a week of waiting, when she felt particularly drained, she went to her room early to get ready for bed. Turning on the light she found a stamped envelope propped against the clock on her dresser—she didn't recognize it so her mother must have put it there. A glance at the return address showed that it came from her father.

She dropped the envelope in the wastebasket started changing clothes. It irritated her when her mother did things like that. A few months ago when the letters started turning up in the mail Jessica asked her mother to put them away in a safe place until she decided whether to read them. She still didn't feel ready, even now—*Why would I want to hear his stupid excuses? Why would I want to make myself even more upset?*—and it only made things worse when her mother tried to push her.

Well, whatever. She'd put the letter where it belonged. Maybe her mother would find it and maybe she wouldn't, and either way Jessica didn't care.

She switched off the light and slid under the covers, snuggling into a comfortable position. She closed her eyes and waited to get drowsy.

It didn't happen. She rolled from side to side and flipped the pillow and adjusted the quilt three or four times, but nothing helped. After half an hour she found herself staring at the ceiling, wide awake. With a disgusted sound she switched on the lamp on the nightstand, squinting against the glare. Then she dug the envelope out of the wastebasket.

Inside was a folded piece of stationary, handwritten on both sides. She opened it and started to read.

HEY THERE KIDDO,

YOU WOULDN'T BELIEVE WHERE I'M WRITING THIS LETTER. I JUST RENTED A HOUSE AT THE BEACH! I'M ON MY BACK PORCH WITH THE WAVES PRACTICALLY LAPPING AT MY FEET. AND TO THINK I DIDN'T HAVE A DIME WHEN I GOT TO FLORIDA! LIKE THEY SAY, BETTER TO BE LUCKY THAN SMART, KNOW WHAT I MEAN?

SO ARE YOU KEEPING THE GRADES UP? REMEMBER,
A FEW YEARS AND YOU'LL BE PREPPING FOR COLLEGE.
DON'T LET UP NOW!

I KEEP WAITING TO HEAR FROM YOU BUT SO FAR
IT'S BEEN A WHOLE LOT OF NOTHING. WOULD IT KILL
YOU TO PICK UP A PHONE ONCE IN A WHILE? OR SEND
A POSTCARD AT LEAST? I PUT OUT ALL THIS EFFORT
AND ALL I GET IS THE SILENT TREATMENT. YOUR
BROTHER PLAYED THAT GAME AND I GOT TIRED OF IT
REAL FAST, LET ME TELL YOU—

Between the furious red haze that blurred Jessica's vision and the crinkling of the paper as her fingers curled into fists, the words had become unreadable. With quick jerking motions she jammed the letter back in the envelope, stuffed it in the trash, and switched off the lamp. In the darkness she pulled her old stuffed koala bear close and curled in a safe spot against the wall, the comforter almost covering her head.

There were many things Jessica didn't understand. She didn't know why her parents had argued so often or why her father had made her happy half the time and frightened the other half; she didn't know what sparked her brother Brad's last fight with their father, when Brad left without a word in the middle of the night; she didn't really know why her father abandoned them a year later, or why his absence made her feel both relieved and ashamed. But one thing seemed obvious: it wasn't fair.

"Other kids have real families," she muttered. "Other kids have real dads. But I don't get one. I don't get one." She squeezed her eyes tight because some part of her was trying to cry, and as usual she wouldn't let it happen.

. . .

Sleep, when it arrived, pulled her somewhere dark and distant, and in the morning she could barely pry her eyes open. She crawled out of bed late, dressed in the same clothes she'd worn yesterday, and dragged herself to the corner just ahead of the bus.

The first class that morning was uneventful. Jessica took a chair near the back and dozed a few times, and the teacher didn't seem to notice. After class she walked to the nearest bathroom and filled a sink with cold water; when it looked deep enough she took a breath and dunked her face. She came up sputtering and gasping and almost felt like she was waking up.

Her second class that day was Biology. As on most days, the class would begin with a meditation, with the students sitting in a circle on the floor. When Jessica arrived she felt relieved to see an open window at the back; the fresh air might clear her head. She took a spot near it and sat down cross-legged.

In the middle of the circle the Biology teacher had arranged some items on a low table: a few oak branches in a vase, with acorns and oak leaves scattered across the tabletop. The teacher's name was Aurora Starchild (she had officially changed it from Carrie Sullivan back in the 1970s). Today she wore a long skirt stitched with American Indian artwork and had woven twigs and leaves into her hair.

"I'll be a few minutes, but don't wait," the teacher said. "Go ahead and find your center." She pressed a button on a CD player and the room echoed with strummed guitar music mingled with the sounds of wind and rain. She dropped some dried leaves onto a saucer and lit them with a match, sending curls of smoke into the air ("for cleansing," she had explained once). Then from the table she picked up a wooden rod and a small bronze bowl that she held on her fingertips. She struck the bowl lightly: *ding*. "Remember," she said, "when we prepare ourselves to learn, when we *desire* to learn, we join with the living energy of the universe. Let's breathe together and feel it flowing in our spines. Ready now: a deep breath in...."

Ding.

"...and out..."

Ding.

"...in..."

Ding.

"...and out..."

Ding.

Jessica breathed along with the bowl and paid attention to her back, trying to feel the energy today. It didn't seem to be working. She thought she might close her eyes to concentrate, or possibly just take a nap, when a movement caught the corner of her eye.

She turned and looked straight into Ariel's face—the girl was leaning over the windowsill from the outside. "Hi!" she said. "Whatcha doing?"

Jessica glanced around the circle; no one had turned to look at them. The teacher struck the bowl again and said, "Now a very *long* breath. Let it fill you all the way down to your toes."

Jessica took a breath to whisper to Ariel but the girl had already climbed through the window. She sat cross-legged next to Jessica, almost bumping the student next to her. None of the other kids seemed to notice.

"Is it always like this at your school?" Ariel said. "I didn't know you got to sit on the floor."

Jessica shook her head, looking at the teacher, who had returned the bowl and rod to the table. "We're going to learn about trees today," the teacher said. "Oak trees. Wonderful, majestic creatures. You can read about them in books, about chlorophyll and stomata and cambium and all those things. But that doesn't tell us what we *really* need to know, does it? Biology is about life, and life is about spirit. We want to understand the life of the tree, the *spirit* of the tree. For that, we must find the answer deep down inside. If we're patient, perhaps we'll understand what it means to *be* a tree."

She took one of the branches from the vase and raised it high. "I want each of you," she intoned, "to imagine you're an acorn."

Ariel leaned closer to Jessica and said, "This is kind of dumb."

Ssshhh, Jessica said, covering it up by clearing her throat. The teacher continued, "Close your eyes now. Picture yourself buried in the ground. The soil is all around you, moist and fertile. Maybe you wait for a long while in the silence and the dark. But then something mysterious happens: your roots begin to grow. You feel them push into the earth, into the dark. They bring you nourishment. You feel yourself filling with life. You need to change, to reach out. You press upward, striving against the earth. And then, all at once...you break free! You stretch out into the light! Ready to grow and become beautiful, just as you were meant to be."

"Okay," Ariel said. "Can we leave? Can we go now?"

Jessica shook her head again. Clearly no one else in the room could see Ariel or hear her voice, but Jessica didn't know how to respond without making a scene. The teacher continued her story, asking everyone to feel their roots sinking deeper and their trunks growing taller, and the seasons pass-ing, and their branches spreading out to the wind and rain. "And when you're strong enough and your branches are wide," she said, "something new happens: you become a home for the birds! They fill your branches and find shelter under your leaves. And they sing! All day long they sing and make their music. You feel like you're holding a symphony in your arms."

Just then Ariel began playing a tune on her pipes. Jessica squeezed her fists—it didn't seem possible no one else would hear it. But the other students kept their eyes shut and didn't react.

Then one of the girls snickered. On the other side a boy snorted and grinned. Around the circle people were sputtering or shaking or otherwise doing their best not to laugh out loud. What was going on? Jessica closed her eyes and listened to Ariel's music—

—and saw a clear picture of a tree with branches bouncing wildly up and down. They bounced because the tree was filled with enormous birds, all flapping and squawking at each other, and when Jessica looked closer she saw that every bird had a face that looked just like the teacher.

"*Stop it!*" Jessica hissed.

In the sudden silence she opened her eyes and found everyone staring at her. She coughed and said, "Excuse me. Sorry." Then with a raised hand: "Umm, Ms. Starchild, could I go to the restroom? I think something's caught in my throat."

"Of course. Do you need any help?" the teacher said.

"No, no, I'll be fine." She pushed herself up and left the room with Ariel right behind. In the safety of the hallway Jessica whispered, "You shouldn't have done that!"

"Why not?" Ariel said, whispering in an exaggerated sort of way, though they both knew it wasn't necessary. "It was funny!"

"You could have got me in trouble!"

"Oh, pooh. Everyone was laughing. You can't get in trouble when everybody likes it."

When they reached the exit door at the end of the hallway Jessica eased it open without making noise. Outside, beyond an open stairwell to the second story, they found a small lawn mostly surrounded by tall shrubs. Walking onto the grass Jessica said, "Sure, it's easy for you, but I'm the one—"

"Okay, okay, I won't do stuff in your class anymore. Promise. Now can we go? It's simple to travel this time, you just—"

"No, not yet. I've got some more questions."

Ariel rolled her eyes. "Oh come *on*—I told you everything already. I don't *know* anything else."

59

"Well, it won't hurt to listen, right? Only take a minute."

Ariel let out a groan and dropped back on the grass with her arms over her head. "Okay, *fine*. But only a minute!"

Jessica dug into a pocket and fished out the folded sheet of paper she'd been carrying for the past week. Opening it she said, "Umm...listen, some of these came from friends of mine, when we talked about you. Is that okay? I mean, that I told them about you?"

Ariel shrugged. "Yeah, I guess."

Jessica waited, then said, "Okay...good." She read from the paper. "First one: *What is the origin of the name 'Ariel,' and does it have any special significance?*"

"*What?*" Ariel said, laughing. "What do you mean?"

"Well, it's like, they want to know if your name is special. Like, does it mean something important?"

"Uh-uh. Don't think so."

"So you don't know anything else about it?"

"What else am I supposed to know?"

Jessica frowned, trying to think of a response. "All right, never mind about that. Here's the next one. *Which of these words would you use to describe yourself: fairy, elf, spirit, angel, genie —*"

Ariel groaned with her hands over her face. "This is taking *forever!* I'm gonna be late if we don't leave right away."

"What...late? For what?"

"For my job today. I have to be on time or it'll get messed up!"

Jessica blinked. "You have a *job?*"

"Of *course* I have a job," Ariel said, rolling her eyes. "What do you think, I just sit and do nothing all day?"

Jessica squinted at her, then looked at the remaining questions.

3. How is it that Jessica can see you when others cannot?

4. *Can you describe your method of "traveling" in more detail?*

5. *How many different worlds are accessible to you?*

6. *When you travel, do you intentionally use mathematics—*

She sighed, sliding the paper back in her pocket. "Okay, let's go."

"Great! Here's what you do." It turned out to be trickier than Ariel seemed to think. Jessica had to stand with her eyes closed while Ariel began a short tune, and on a particular note she turned quickly to the right. On her first attempt she missed the beat and almost fell over; on the second try she got it right, the air quivering around her as it had the last time they traveled.

Opening her eyes, she found they were standing on a sidewalk. It looked like an ordinary sidewalk, running alongside a normal-looking suburban street with houses on both sides. The green lawns looked well-tended and trees were evenly spaced in the parkways. The air felt cooler than it had been at the school.

"Where is this?" Jessica said.

"Somewhere in your world—in the regular world," Ariel said. "Not sure where exactly."

A woman in a damp exercise outfit came jogging up the sidewalk, puffing rather loudly. Jessica murmured, "She's not going to see you, right? You're still invisible?"

"Yup. So are you, I think."

"What—me?"

The woman drew close and they stepped off the sidewalk to let her pass. As a test Jessica waved and said, "Good morning." The woman jogged by without a glance.

Out in the street two boys were approaching, one riding a bike and the other a skateboard. Jessica stepped off the curb, waving her arms and calling "Hey! Hey! Come here a second!"

The boys paid no attention, passing two feet away without interrupting their conversation.

"Whoa," Jessica said, watching them go. "That's really weird."

"It's the traveling that does it, I think," Ariel said. "It's like we're not totally here, just sort of in-between. That's how I think of it anyway."

From the house behind them they heard a *whomp* like a door slamming, followed by two loud voices talking over each other. Ariel said, "I'd better get started," and walked up the lawn toward the house.

Keeping pace with her Jessica said, "So, what's going to happen?"

"Well, two married people live here. They have a kid, too, a little boy, but he's not here this morning. The man's name is Eric and the woman is Marisha. They're having an argument right now."

"Yeah, I kind of figured. What are you supposed to do?"

"I have to hide their car keys."

Jessica wrinkled her face. "Car keys? Why are you doing that?"

Ariel shrugged. "I don't know."

Jessica watched her, waiting for some other response. She sighed. "Well...I guess we'll see what happens."

"Yup."

They had reached the porch, a concrete pad in front of a door made of painted wood with a narrow glass window. Before Jessica could ask how Ariel planned to enter the house, the girl stepped up and rang the doorbell.

The voices inside fell off and Jessica heard footsteps. Ariel said, "Oh, something else. I don't think you should touch anything."

"Oh? What do you mean?"

"Well, you probably shouldn't pick stuff up or move things

around. I can do that sometimes when I do a job. But it might be bad if you did it."

Jessica wanted to ask exactly what *bad* meant, but just then the door pulled open. Inside stood a man of average height who looked about thirty years old; he wore a dark t-shirt and khaki work pants with paint stains on one side. He poked his head out the doorway and looked one way and then another, making a disgusted face. "No one's here!" he yelled over his shoulder. "Neighbor kids are playing tricks again!"

"Now," Ariel said, and she slipped past the man into the house. Jessica jumped to follow, skipping under the man's arm before he closed the door. She found Ariel pressed up against a wall and she joined her as the man walked into a high-ceilinged hall that stretched towards the back.

"Now what?" Jessica said.

"Well—" Ariel said, just as a woman stormed from the back of the house. She wore short pants and a button-up shirt, and in one hand she gripped a printed sheet of paper.

"See? Right there!" she yelled at the man, jabbing a finger at the paper. "*Right there!* Like I said!"

"This is *ridiculous*," he said. "It's so *stupid*."

"Yeah, it's stupid because the money's gone! Like you dumped it in the drain!"

"Put it away, it's not the point."

"It's all screwed up and it's your fault!"

"Yeah, so when did you get so helpless?" he said. "Like you can't make a couple phone calls?"

"Now you listen, I'm taking care of Michael every day—"

"Like I'm not working? Like I'm not there ten hours—"

"—and at night, when you don't want to, and nobody else—"

"—and you don't listen, you just walk in here—"

"—I've had it, just had it, and you're not even—"

They somehow made their way down the hall, both talking

at the tops of their voices, neither seeming to hear what the other was saying. Jessica said, "Umm...Eric and Marisha, right?"

"Uh-huh."

"It's crazy. They act like bratty kids. You'd think people wouldn't do that after they grew up."

"Yeah. I can't even tell what they're arguing about."

"Me neither." Looking around, Jessica said, "So, do you know where the car keys are?"

"Nope, I gotta find them. You can help if you want."

Against one wall in the hallway, two narrow tables held a collection of houseplants, photos, and knickknacks; Jessica and Ariel searched them quickly without finding any keys. On the left side of the hall a staircase climbed to the second story, and to the right an archway opened into another room. Jessica nodded at the arch and said, "Let's try there next."

On the other side they found a crowded living room, packed with furniture that looked clean and modern and thoroughly uncomfortable. After looking around for a few moments Ariel pointed to a coffee table. "Look—those are car keys, right?"

"Yeah—they're like others I've seen, anyway," Jessica said. "So now what? Do you take them somewhere?"

"No. I'll play some music, but only when the people are in the room."

They sat on the edge of a sofa near the table and listened to the argument as it rose and fell. Before long, Eric's voice came louder and clearer. "Where'd you put the keys *this* time?" he yelled, and Marisha responded, "They're in the living room, right where you dropped them!"

Jessica heard footfalls, and when Eric walked through the archway she said "Now." Ariel began to play. The tune felt light and meandering, a melody that seemed to wander from place to place without a recurring pattern. Jessica knew the music wasn't meant for her but she still felt lightheaded as she listened.

Eric stalked through the room, looking at tabletops and shelves and the mantle above the fireplace, then stopped beside the coffee table where the keys were lying. He made a sputtering sound and threw his arms in the air. "They're not here!" he yelled.

Marisha stepped into the room. "They were there, on the table. What did you do with them?"

"Oh, right," he said, "it's *my* fault. *You* never make a mistake. *You* never lose anything."

"They're not my keys. If *yours* are lost, guess who lost them?"

"I'm not going to miss this," he said, following Marisha as she left the room. "Not gonna miss it at *all*."

Watching them go, Jessica said, "You know what? I think I know why you're doing this."

"Really?"

"This might be bigger than an argument. It sounds like maybe Eric wants to leave Marisha."

"Oh, yeah?"

"Yeah. But he couldn't find the keys so he can't go, at least right away. And if he can't leave maybe they'll both calm down, and maybe he'll think it over—"

There was a loud *bang* like someone slamming a hand into a cupboard. "Forget it!" Eric yelled. "I'll get the other keys upstairs and I'm gone!"

Jessica and Ariel turned to each other and said "Uh-oh" at nearly the same moment. They jumped from the couch and ran to the hallway, racing up the stairs to the second story landing. At the top, a little out of breath, Jessica looked over the railing. "He's not coming yet," she said. "But which room should we...."

Her voice trailed off. To her right in one of the open doorways, she saw something strange: a small oddly-shaped thing about three feet tall, standing motionless with one hand grasping the doorjamb. It had lumpish gray body with a bulbous head and pencil-thin arms and legs. At first glance Jessica thought it must be a kind of toy, an ugly goblin doll meant to startle people when they happened to see it. But then the thing sniffed the air, blinked at her, and stuck out its tongue.

Jessica stepped back. "Ariel," she coughed, pointing at the thing, "Ariel—what *is* that?"

The girl turned. "Oh—a spud. Don't worry about it."

"A *what*?"

"A spud. You see them sometimes when you're in-between. Don't worry, it won't bother us."

"But how do you—hey! Did you see that? That was gross!" The creature had made a rude gesture, and now it was sticking out its tongue again and waggling its hands beside its ears. Ariel stepped toward it while she played a high piercing trill on her pipes. The creature squealed and fell over with its hands clapped to its ears, then skittered on all fours back into the room behind it.

"See?" Ariel said. "No big deal."

"Yeah, right," Jessica said, catching her breath. "Is there anything *else* you haven't told me?"

Heavy footsteps echoed in the stairwell; Jessica looked down and saw Eric pounding up the stairs two at a time. "So, what now?" she said. "Should we find the other keys?"

"Nope. I have a different idea."

They moved aside as Eric reached the top and then slipped in behind him when he turned into one of the rooms. The room looked like an office or a den, with bookshelves on one side and two cluttered computer desks on the other. Eric opened a top drawer on one of the desks and reached a hand inside.

Ariel began to play, a different tune than the one she had

played downstairs; the melody seemed simple but it looped back again and again as though spinning in a circle. Eric's expression turned confused and he stopped rummaging in the drawer. "Crap," he muttered. "What was I looking for?" He poked through a few more items, frowning. "I hate it when I do that. So why did I come up here?" He turned to the other desk, lifting papers and moving books, trying to jog his memory.

Jessica allowed herself to relax; it looked like this might actually work. Eric closed the desk drawer, shaking his head as though he were ready to give up. Then through a window that overlooked the front lawn Jessica heard a faint clinking noise – she couldn't hear clearly over Ariel's piping but it almost sounded like rattling keys.

Stepping around Eric she looked out the window. She saw a narrow walkway leading from the porch to a driveway where a car was parked. Marisha was halfway to the car with a set of keys in her hand. "Ariel," Jessica said, "Marisha's outside, and she's got keys!"

Ariel broke off the music. "This is nuts. How many have they got?" They ran from the room, slipping and jumping down the stairs and then out through the wide-open front door. They turned toward the driveway, but too late: Marisha had already unlocked the door on the driver's side.

"Oh, this is terrible," Ariel said.

"Can't you do something, still?" Jessica said. "Could you make her lock the door again?"

"No. I can make people feel things but I can't make them do things. It doesn't work like that."

Marisha pulled the door wide and tossed the keys onto the front seat. Walking back to the house she cupped her hands around her mouth and called, "Hey! I took care of it for you! You can split any time you want!"

Jessica wrinkled her nose, saying, "I got an idea." She stepped to the inside of the car door, looking over the knobs until she found the lock button. "Is it okay for you to touch the car?" she said.

"Yeah, I'm pretty sure."

"Then I think you can lock the keys inside."

"Really?"

"Uh-huh. First push that knob, with the red mark on it." Ariel pressed it until it clicked in place.

"Now you just shut the door. I hope." With the car parked uphill Ariel only had to nudge the outside of the door; it picked up speed until it closed with a satisfying *chunk*.

Marisha was waiting when Eric walked out of the house. "You're all set, don't even thank—" She broke off when they approached the car.

"What happened?" Eric said. "You didn't lock them inside, did you?"

They peered through the windshield at the keys lying on the seat. Marisha tried the door handle but it wouldn't open. "Oh, perfect," Eric said.

"It was open when I left it."

"So it closed by itself, is that it?"

They stared at the car looking tired and defeated, as though they had no energy left for this kind of a problem. Marisha said, "We could break a window."

"Costs about three hundred bucks to fix."

"Then we'd better call somebody, I guess."

"Yeah," Eric said, and he walked inside to call a locksmith. Marisha lowered herself to the edge of the front porch, letting out a frustrated sigh and rubbing her forehead with one hand.

Jessica said, "Should we wait to see what happens?" and Ariel nodded. They sat on a dry area of the lawn not far from the porch.

Eric returned and leaned against a post on the porch. "They'll be here in about an hour," he said.

They watched cars passing on the street. Eric took a tired

breath. "Guess I wasn't supposed to leave today."

"Yeah," Marisha said. "Or maybe you didn't want to, really."

"Or maybe *you* didn't want me to."

She shrugged. "I was thinking about my parents. They argued a lot—I mean *a lot* —but it never felt dangerous to me. I never felt like they were splitting up. They knew how to fight without fighting, maybe? I was wondering how they did that, for so many years."

"Maybe it's something you learn when you grow up."

"Yeah. So when will we do that?"

"Beats me."

After another silence, Eric said, "You want a drink?" and Marisha said, "Sure." He turned back inside while Marisha got up to follow.

Jessica let out a *huh.* "Hey, I think you did it."

"Hope so," Ariel said. "But you did most of it, not me."

"No way, you were the one. I just watched most of the time." Jessica leaned back on her elbows, relaxing on the cool grass in the warm sunlight. It felt good to sit there knowing that she might have actually done something useful that morning. "So, is this what you do all the time? You help people like this?"

Ariel blew on a dandelion puffball that she'd picked from the lawn. "Oh, I do lots of different stuff. Sometimes it works out but not always. Sometimes it's hard to tell."

Jessica lay back and watched the drifting seeds. "Maybe you should've been around my family awhile back."

"Why's that?"

"My parents had fights like that, only lots worse. They'd go at it for hours at night and I'd barely get any sleep."

"Wow, that's awful."

"Yeah. My dad drank a lot, and maybe that's why it happened. But sometimes he said he only drank because they fought. I never understood it. About a year ago he just left us, and they got a divorce. He went off to Florida."

"Oh, I'm sorry. Sounds really sad."

Jessica shrugged and spoke in her mature, reasonable voice. "I'm mostly okay with it now. Lots of kids at school have parents who split up and it almost feels normal. It's quieter at home when it's just me and my mom, so maybe I'm better off."

Ariel nodded. "Yeah, but it still hurts, right? I bet it hurts a *lot*."

Jessica felt her throat tighten. She tried to think of something to say, then realized she didn't feel like talking anymore. Sitting up she said, "You know, it's been a long time since we got here. Should we leave now?"

"I don't need to hurry."

"Yeah, but I've got more classes at school. I shouldn't wait."

"Okay, if that's it." They stood and walked back to the sidewalk while Ariel explained how the traveling would work: she would play nearly the same tune as before, but Jessica had to turn a different direction on another beat of the music. Just as Ariel was ready to play, Jessica remembered something she'd wondered about.

"I was gonna ask—how do you get the jobs, or where do they come from? Like, does someone give them to you?"

"Yup," Ariel said. "Mr. Peabody."

Jessica blinked. "Mr. Peabody?"

"Uh-huh."

"Well...is that someone I should know?"

Ariel shook her head, looking oddly uncomfortable. "I don't think so, he's nice and he's helped me a lot, but he's, umm... kinda boring, most of the time. I don't think you'd want to meet him."

"Oh."

"Is that okay?"

"Well, yeah. It's just...I was hoping this would start making sense, sooner or later. But never mind, let's just go home."

Chapter 5

The Grieving King

"*MR. PEABODY?*" Mitch said.

Jessica sighed. "Yes. That's what she said."

Mitch and Mr. McNulty looked at each other. They had gathered again in the library room at the McNultys' home, sitting on some battered folding chairs near the bay window. Outside the day was fading and the late light cast an amber hue on everyone's faces. Jessica had returned from her trip with Ariel just a few hours before.

"That's *exactly* what she said?" Mitch asked.

"Yes, exactly," Jessica said, somewhat annoyed. "I'm just telling you what happened, you know, I can't help how it sounds."

"Yeah, okay, I get it."

Mitch and Mr. McNulty looked at each other again. Jessica asked, "Would this be a good time for some more research?"

"Well..." Mr. McNulty drawled, "I got a hunch it wouldn't do us a whole lot of good, at the moment. Your friend seems to enjoy keeping us confused."

"Yeah. She's good at that."

Mr. McNulty took off his glasses and cleaned them with a

handkerchief. "Probably the best bet right now is to go back to our first questions. So let's start with the 'traveling.' You find out anything new this time?"

"One thing was different," Jessica said. "I didn't need to make a picture in my head. But Ariel said we didn't leave this world, so I suppose it was a shorter trip. Maybe that made the difference?"

"Could be," Mitch said. "If you don't travel as far, the 'formula,' or whatever it is, might be simpler."

"So it fits, for now," said Mr. McNulty. "We'll see what happens next time. Now the other one: who or what is Ariel? We make any progress?"

"Not much, sorry," Jessica said. "I didn't get very far when I tried to go through the list."

"No problem. If the girl won't sit for it, we'll try something else."

"Well, I've got a question," Mitch said, tapping a sketch that Jessica had drawn, a pencil outline of the creature she'd seen in the doorway. "Ariel called this thing a 'spud.' But that doesn't tell you anything about it, you know? It's like a nickname kids would pick if they saw what it looked like. And it's kind of the same with 'Mr. Peabody.' The name doesn't tell you anything except that it sounds funny, like a name from a TV show."

"Yeah, that's true," Jessica said.

"So, I'm wondering, are we expecting too much? From Ariel, I mean? She does all those amazing things so we figure she has to understand stuff better than we do. But what if that's not true? Maybe she doesn't have the answers we want. It's kind of crazy, but maybe she just does what she does and doesn't think much about it."

Jessica considered it. "Actually, that kind of fits. Ariel must've said 'I don't know' about half the time when I managed to ask a question. I never thought she was trying to fool me—

she just didn't know. And she didn't seem to *care* that she didn't know."

"Interesting," Mr. McNulty said. "And peculiar. If that's her attitude, how did she ever learn to do what she does?"

"Maybe she learned them from Mr. Peabody," Jessica said.

"Whoever, or whatever, he is," Mitch said.

"Right."

They were quiet until Mitch said, "If there's nothing else, we could add a question to the list: *Who is Mr. Peabody?* Since he might be the key to the whole thing."

"Makes sense," Jessica said.

"Done, then," Mr. McNulty said. "Jessica, you said your friend would be back in about three days?"

"Yes—she said she'll have another job, and she'll meet me at school like before. I'll try to squeeze in some more questions. Want to get together again after that?"

"You know where to find me," Mr. McNulty said.

The next few days passed without much trouble. Jessica didn't feel nearly as anxious as she had the last time Ariel was away; the girl clearly knew how to find her, and Jessica saw no reason to doubt that she would return right about the time she said she would. If the waiting wasn't completely painless, it was certainly bearable.

At home, her mother didn't try to start any awkward conversations, and if anything she seemed more subdued than usual. On the third evening, though, Jessica noticed something odd: her mother kept carrying the handset from their cordless telephone, keeping it nearby while she worked in the kitchen or sat in the living room. Her mother didn't enjoy talking on the phone at night—she tried to avoid it, usually—and Jessica felt puzzled until she looked at the wall calendar near the refrigerator. The date had been circled in red; it was the anniversary of her brother's disappearance. Brad had run away exactly two years ago. Her mother was hoping he would finally decide to call.

Jessica didn't mention her discovery since her mother rarely talked about that sort of thing. She said goodnight at the usual time, went to her room, got ready for bed, and crawled under the covers. Turning to the wall next to Brad's old room she placed a hand flat against it, straining again to hear the sounds he used to make in the evenings. The room was silent as always.

"You should call," Jessica whispered. "Mom really misses you. You should call and tell her you're all right."

After a time, she added, "And I need to talk to you. I could tell you my problems and you could say *What a mess you got into,* or *Use your brains, silly,* or *Let me fix it for you.* Like old times. And then everything would be okay. Just call, please?"

On nights like this one, after all the distractions of the day had fallen away, she could practically taste the emptiness on the other side of the wall. Her brother's absence became tangible, like a weight around her heart. Just now, in her mind, the features of his room shrank and faded away, leaving little more than a blank space, a widening darkness. Too big for her to fight. Almost big enough to fall into and disappear.

She squeezed her eyes shut and whispered through clenched teeth. "You don't know how much this hurts. You just don't know."

She lay awake, silent and listening. The telephone in the kitchen did not ring before she fell asleep.

The next day at school, the first few periods passed in a blur and Jessica didn't feel completely awake until almost noon. When the lunch bell rang she got her bag from her hall locker and walked to the quad near the cafeteria. Most days she sat outside with Mitch, but he was skipping lunch that day to finish a project in his Physics class. She found an empty bench beside a wide green lawn and sat down to eat by herself.

After two bites of her sandwich, she heard a familiar voice: "Hi! Ready to go?" She turned and looked into Ariel's face; the girl was standing oddly close, as usual. Jessica continued chewing, then swallowed. Under her breath she said, "Okay if I finish my lunch?"

Ariel said "Sure" and plopped down on the bench. She looked around at the lawn and the other kids in the lunch area, swinging her legs under the bench because her feet didn't quite touch the ground. Her feet were still bare and she still wore the same cut-off jeans and shirt she'd been wearing the first day they met.

"So...you want something to eat?" Jessica said.

"Nah. No thanks."

"But you eat, right? You eat food?"

"Sure. Once in a while. Not very often."

"Oh." Before Jessica could ask anything else Ariel pointed toward the middle of the lawn and said, "What are those kids doing?"

Out on the grass, several students were walking single-file with large gaps between them. They had all dressed identically in brown pants and large white shirts that billowed when the breeze blew. They held their arms away from their bodies and walked with slow cumbersome movements, weaving slightly from side to side.

"Oh them," Jessica said. "They're from one of the American History classes. The one with, umm...Mr. Schumacher."

"Oh. Okay."

"His classes are—different. Like sometimes he has people do pantomimes or act out the stuff they're learning. It's supposed to help you understand the history lessons. Or make them more real. Or something."

"Oh. So, what are those kids doing?"

"Well, they've been learning about the Westward Expansion. Pioneers and stuff," Jessica said. "So I think they're, umm...pretending to be covered wagons."

On the lawn the line of walkers began swinging around in a slow curve, gradually forming into a circle. One of the girls sat down in the center and began flicking her hands in the air like the flames of a campfire.

Ariel watched with narrowed eyes. "I was wondering," she said, "are all the schools around here like this one?"

Jessica sighed. "No. Esterhaus is...special."

"Oh."

"So, should we go to your job now?"

"Sure."

They left the lunch area and climbed some concrete steps to a main walkway. Jessica was heading for a quiet spot where they could travel without being seen, but she took a long route, hoping to ask questions on the way. When they turned a corner into an empty hall, she said, "The job today, it's from Mr. Peabody again?"

"Yep."

"How long have you been doing work for him?"

"Oh, a long time."

"Does he, like, pay you for it?"

Ariel laughed. "No, silly. I'm just helping. He helped me so I'm helping him."

"Oh." Jessica pondered that. "Did he teach you to do the things you do? The traveling, and playing the music?"

"Oh, no. He's taught me stuff, but I knew the traveling and all before he rescued me."

"Rescued...? What do you mean?"

"I mean, found me. Not rescued. Not really." She looked uncomfortable again. "Are we close to where we're going? This is taking a long time."

A few kids stepped out of a room just in front of them and

Jessica kept quiet as they exited the hall onto an outdoor walkway. It led to the spot Jessica had picked out, a small lawn behind a maintenance building. When they reached it, Ariel explained how the traveling would work: Jessica wouldn't have to perform any movements this time but she had to make a new picture in her head. "It's like a coffee cup, only tall and skinny," Ariel said. "With a handle on the side. And it has to be dark red, like a brick."

Lots of numbers in there, Mitch would say, Jessica thought. *We might be going a long way.* She closed her eyes and pictured the odd coffee cup while Ariel played a high, lonely-sounding trill on her pipes. Jessica felt the ground slide and stretch under her feet until it abruptly snapped back into place.

Opening her eyes, she saw nothing but gray. She blinked a few times and realized they were standing in a mist, a pale fog that flowed over them in long translucent wisps. Beneath her feet she could see a platform made of wooden timbers; the wood looked rough-hewn and seemed to be coated with tar. "Where are we?" she said.

"It's a castle," Ariel said. "We're on top of one of the towers."

"Oh. Cool."

The fog thinned in front of them, revealing the outline of a curved stone wall several feet away. The wall had gaps or slits spaced along its length, just like in pictures of castles that Jessica had seen. (*Battlements*—that's what they called the gap-toothed walls. She remembered the word from Mr. McNulty's class.) Near the wall a trap door opened into the platform, with faint yellow light flickering from below.

"That's the stairs," Ariel said. She led the way as they stepped into the opening. A stone staircase spiraled down the inside of the tower, each step anchored between the outer wall and a central pillar. The stairs had a steep pitch and Jessica kept a hand on the pillar to steady herself as they descended.

"So, what are you supposed to do here?" she said.

"It's kind of complicated," Ariel said. "But the main thing is, a war might be starting tonight. Some people here want to stop it and I'm supposed to help them."

"Oh...can you do that?"

"I hope so."

At every half-turn small oil lamps flared in niches in the wall, giving them just enough light to see the steps. By the time they reached the doorway at the bottom Jessica had gotten dizzy from the descent.

They stepped out of the stairwell into a hall or corridor lit by torches set in brackets in the walls. The air felt warm and dense, rich with smoky scents of spices and cooked meat. From the left a few boys hurried by, carrying trays burdened with cooked foods. The boys looked red-faced and anxious and their clothes seemed both elegant and archaic, like costumes from a Renaissance Fair or a movie set in the Middle Ages.

"Whoa. This is interesting," Jessica said.

"Yeah. I didn't know guys could wear long stockings like that."

A few more boys rushed past with their trays, and off to the left a huge man stepped out of a doorway. He waved a long knife in the air and yelled at the boys while sweat dripped from his face onto his dirty apron. He was clearly upset but he spoke a language Jessica had never heard before.

"Do you understand what he's saying? I sure don't," she said.

"Oh, I almost forgot. Look here a minute." Ariel stepped close and squinted into her eyes. She raised her pipes and began playing a complex tune, starting low and quickly spiraling higher and higher until it was almost inaudible. The hairs on Jessica's neck and arms prickled and her head spun; she reached for the wall to steady herself. Then—

"—and no more thieving from the trays or I'll skin you with my own hands!" the man roared. "You can pick through the leftovers when the gentlefolk are drunk and sleeping!" Then he stomped back through the doorway.

"Oh," Jessica said. "That worked. Umm...thanks."

"No problem. So, now we need to find the big room where people are having a feast."

Off to the right a large double doorway spilled out light and noise in equal measure, and boys carrying food scurried through it as they watched. "Looks like that's the place," Jessica said.

Passing through the doorway they entered a room as big as a church and as noisy as a football stadium. It was lit by candles and torches and a roaring fireplace built into a wall—a fireplace so huge that a grown man could have walked into it. Long tables lined both sides of the room and crowds of people sat on benches at the tables, eating servings of bread and meat pies and cooked vegetables from wooden platters.

The people at those tables were dressed plainly, for the most part, and to Jessica's eyes their manners seemed remarkably bad. They handled all of their food with bare fingers, including the cooked meat, often tossing bones and scraps on the floor and letting the wandering dogs fight for them. At every table people talked or even yelled through mouthfuls of food, making a racket worse than a school cafeteria at lunch hour.

A few serving boys ran back to the doorway, and when Jessica stepped out of their way she got a clearer view of the head table, set on a raised platform at the far end of the room. White linens draped that table and the vessels on it flashed gold and silver in the firelight. The people sitting there appeared both richer and more refined than the people on the floor. The women wore long-sleeved gowns of deep greens and blues and shades of cinnamon and rose, and the men, with clothing nearly as colorful, wore dark cloaks fastened at the shoulder with heavy brooches.

Ariel tugged on Jessica's sleeve and said, "See the two people in the middle? That's the king and queen." Jessica had already noticed them, sitting below a scarlet canopy trimmed in gold. The man had a short gray beard and wore a gold band around his forehead. He seemed sad and distant, eating only some fragments of bread, mostly deaf to the voices around him. The woman looked equally sad but more attentive, speaking quietly to a few people close by. As Jessica watched she turned to her husband and touched his hand; he gave her a shadow of a smile but the sorrow in his eyes did not lift.

"They're not very happy," Jessica said.

"It's because of their son. He died just a few weeks ago."

"Oh, that's terrible. No wonder."

"Yeah. I need to tell you the whole story, but first things first. I should do something about the spuds."

"What spuds?" Jessica said, but then looking around the room she saw what Ariel was talking about. Odd-looking creatures ran here and there across the floor, scrambling on all fours and annoying some of the larger dogs, who barked and snapped at them. (Apparently the dogs could see them even if the people couldn't.) Some smaller spuds crawled along the tabletops or sat on the mantle. A tall spindly one had even settled onto the canopy over the king; Jessica had thought it was a kind of decoration.

"Yuck," Jessica said, shuddering. "They're all over the place. I didn't notice."

"They hang around a lot when bad things are happening," Ariel said. "I think maybe it attracts them. Wait here a minute and I'll take care of it."

She made her way to the middle of the room, skipping around a serving boy and dodging a large bone tossed from the tables. When she reached the center, she raised her pipes and played a long undulating tone; the spuds stopped what they were doing and covered their ears, rolling on the ground and yowling like cats. Ariel played another note and the yowling got louder. She played a sharp trill as she spun around on one foot, and every spud spun in place along with her. Then she played a note that started high and climbed higher until it was almost painful, even in Jessica's ears. That did the trick: the spuds leapt up and scattered out through the various doorways—all except for a pair on the mantelpiece, who dropped to the ground spitting and hissing before they skittered up the inside of the chimney.

"That's better," Ariel said when she returned. "It's easy when there aren't too many."

"Oh," Jessica said. Seeing the spuds in the room had given her an odd feeling of revulsion, almost a kind of nausea, and she was more than a little happy to see them go. "What do you do when there's too many?"

"Just be more careful. Anyway, let's get out of the way and I'll tell you what's going on." As they moved closer to the fireplace she said, "First of all, this castle is in a kingdom called Longmarch. There's another kingdom nearby called Crannocmere. I don't know why, but the two kingdoms have been fighting each other for a long time. The king here, the king of Longmarch, decided he wanted to make peace, and he worked at it for years. He finally got the other king to sign a treaty and right after that they had a big festival to celebrate."

"Well, that's good."

"Yeah, but then something bad happened. The king and queen here had a son, Prince Harold. He was like eighteen years old. At the festival, he was drinking and horsing around with some knights from Crannocmere, and he accidentally got stabbed, and the next day he died."

"Oh, wow."

"Yeah. And the king and queen don't have any other kids. The whole kingdom was in mourning for weeks. This is the first big meal they've had since Harold died."

"That's awful," Jessica said. "No wonder they're so sad."

"Uh-huh. Now the problem is, some people here want the king to take revenge on Crannocmere. A few of them never liked the treaty and they want to use this to start the fighting again."

"So, what does the king think?"

"Nobody's sure. But the bad people think he's ready to listen to them. There, you see that guy?" She pointed to a man sitting a couple places away from the king; he wore an embroidered tunic made of dark blue velvet and his mustache was carefully trimmed. "That's the Lord Chamberlain. He's giving a speech a little later. He wants to get everybody riled up and maybe demand that the king start the war again."

"That doesn't sound good. But what are you supposed to do?"

"Stop him, somehow," Ariel said, shrugging.

"But how can you—" Jessica broke off when she saw a man stand up from one of the long tables. His arms were muscled like a football player's and the left side of his head had a patch of bare skin where a long scar ran up past his hairline. He lifted a metal goblet in one hand and pounded a fist on the table.

"A toast!" he called in a coarse voice. "A toast for Harold!" Around the room others called out "A toast! A toast!" and some of the noise fell away. The man bowed briefly to the king's table and said, "Your majesties. Lords. Ladies. And all good folk here assembled. I raise a cup to Prince Harold, the bravest young man that ever took up sword in Longmarch. I was proud to be his swordmaster, proud to ride beside him in battle, prouder still to be his liegeman. He was the best of us all. God keep him in his peace. God keep us all in his peace."

"*Hear, hear,*" people called, and they all took long drinks from their cups. Ariel leaned to Jessica and said, "That guy is Renard. He's a knight, and so are the others at that table. He thinks it's wrong to start fighting Crannocmere again now that there's a treaty. Most of the knights feel the same way."

"Oh?" Jessica said. "Can't they just say they won't do it?"

"Uh-uh. They do what the king tells them. That's the way it is when you're a knight."

Another man stood up from the same table. He seemed nearly Renard's equal in size but his eyes blinked in a blurry sort of way and he looked wobbly on his feet. "A toast, everyone...a toast to Harold," he said, lifting his cup. "A great prince. A good friend. We'll miss him horribly. All of us. A good friend. And he could hold his drink. Bottoms up." He tipped his head far back to drain his cup and would have fallen over backwards if other men had not caught him.

Laughter and cheering broke out around the room, and as it died, Jessica noticed the Chamberlain rising at the head table. His eyes surveyed the room as he straightened his sleeves, and he raised his own goblet, a bright silver cup ornamented with gold. "A toast," he called in a clear voice, "a toast to Harold and the kingdom he loved so dearly."

To Jessica's surprise a few people began hissing; she turned to ask Ariel about it but found she'd slipped away. She spotted her sitting on the front of the platform not far from the Chamberlain. The girl was watching him closely and tapping a few fingers on her pipes, but she didn't seem ready to play.

The Chamberlain, meanwhile, paid no attention to the noises in the hall. He bowed to the king and the rest of the room, saying, "Your majesties, my lords and ladies, and gentlefolk all. I beg to speak of Harold, the flower of Longmarch, the jewel of the realm. There is no pain like the pain we feel at his loss. It is a wound in all of our souls, a wound that bleeds and does not heal. And wounded as well, I fear, is the honor of our fair kingdom. In truth the honor of Longmarch has been stolen, as surely as Harold's life was stolen away before its time. It falls to us now, as a calling and a duty, to regain that honor, no matter the sorrow, no matter the cost."

His voice felt warm, caring, and persuasive, and Jessica didn't trust him for a minute. He reminded her of politicians or salesmen she'd seen on television, the kind that tell you everything you want to hear but don't mean a word of it. And it seemed that others in the room shared her doubts. The knight Renard spoke up in a loud voice.

"We know what Harold wanted," he said. "He wanted us to keep our word and keep the treaty. Is that what you want, Chamberlain? Tell us plainly, so we can all hear it."

"Sir, your concern flatters me," the Chamberlain said. "But surely my wishes are of no account when the fate of the realm weighs upon us. Let us ask instead, what does duty demand when our honor is threatened? How would Harold have risen to defend it, young Harold who loved Longmarch more than us all? Would any sacrifice have been too great? The answer is plain enough for any man."

Renard's face wore a dark expression but he did not respond. Another voice spoke from another table, even drunker than the knight who had given the toast. "Ahh, siddown, Chamberlain!" the man yelled. "Your words ain't fit for pigs!"

Some in the audience laughed or jeered, but the Chamberlain did not miss a beat. "Well spoken, good sire," he said with a nod. "And if my words are not fit for pigs, by all means I must urge you to cover your ears."

Laughter and foot-stomping erupted from the tables. Several of those near the drunken man slapped his back and made snorting noises; he seemed pleased with the attention but uncertain what the ruckus was about. Over the applause, the Chamberlain continued, "We have always loved a good jest, and well that we should. But we have not come together this night for merriment alone, have we? No, certainly not. A grave duty has fallen upon our kingdom, whether we will it or not. Tonight, we must gather the strength to shoulder this burden, for the memory of young Harold and the glory of Longmarch."

He spoke on in much the same manner, calm and reassuring. He praised the grandeur of the kingdom and the courage of the king and the bravery of his knights. He recalled tales from the past, of heroes and warriors who arose in times of need to strike back at their enemies. He spoke sadly of kingdoms that had lost their honor when they lost their will. He never once uttered the word *revenge*, but again and again Jessica felt it pulsing under his voice, as firm and steady as a heartbeat.

And the longer he spoke the more it seemed the crowd was coming to his side. People began to cheer when he named famous victories and favorite heroes, or when he described enemies fleeing in defeat. A few called out "All for Longmarch!" and "Harold! For Harold!" Most of the knights did not join the fervor, but Jessica could see that they were in no mood to stop it; the Chamberlain's words had overwhelmed them like all the rest.

Jessica felt the speech building to a climax. The people's cheers grew louder and more frequent. The Chamberlain's voice rose in power. And still Ariel did nothing: she sat in the same spot, staring intently and blowing idly on her pipes. Did she even have a plan? If she did, was there enough time to make a difference?

"I ask you all," the Chamberlain rang out, "where is the realm more blest than our own? In all the wide world, is there a land more favored than fair Longmarch?"

NO, came the answer from dozens of voices.

"With a dark time upon us, shall we turn aside? Shall we flee like children and fly our shame like a banner, mocked and mourned before the world?"

NO, came the answer.

"Then shall we stand firm? Shall we join our hearts with

85

those who came before, daring in the face of danger, valiant in deed, rich in glory?"

YES! came the answer.

"Shall we pledge our strength and our courage and rise as one against our foes?"

YES! came the answer.

"Then, brave people, with souls forged like iron and hearts bright as steel, let us vow together, let us vow in this moment —" Ariel played a sudden sharp note on her pipes, and the Chamberlain coughed. He cleared his throat and said, "I say, let us vow together, as one—" Ariel played the note and he coughed again. "As I say, we shall—*cough*—we shall vow —*cough, cough*—"

Chuckles rose from the benches. The Chamberlain cleared his throat, said "Your pardon, please," and reached for his goblet; Ariel jumped to her feet and stepped to the edge of the table. When the Chamberlain lifted the cup to his lips, she stood high on her toes, reached across the table, and bumped her fist into the Chamberlain's elbow.

Wine spilled around the edges of the cup and poured down the man's chin. Several more people laughed and hooted. The Chamberlain looked sharply at the man to his right (the man seemed surprised and shook his head), but kept his composure. Reaching into a sleeve he drew out a handkerchief and dabbed the corners of his mouth. "So, we see how a man stumbles when he stands alone," he said, lowering the goblet to the table. "How much more surely must we stand together, when our enemies strike without warning, when they stab us to the heart—"

Lying on the Chamberlain's platter was a long-handled knife; Ariel's hand darted out and pushed it a few inches. When the base of the goblet dropped onto the handle the knife cata-pulted, spraying bits of potato and sausage across the Chamberlain's face. The goblet meanwhile fell forward and spilled dark red wine down the front of the tablecloth.

The laughter came louder then, mixed with some applause and cheers, and for the first time a spark of anger lit the Chamberlain's eyes. Ariel stepped back from the table and began playing an odd tune, a low rumbling sound that didn't seem to vary or progress. She kept playing as the Chamberlain dabbed his face and spoke again.

"There are some, I fear, who have no care for the trial that is upon us," he declared. "There are some who find it a sport, a matter for jesting. To that I say but one thing, and one thing alone...." At that moment Ariel ended the rumbling tones with a final sharp note, a tiny *pop*.

The Chamberlain let out an enormous belch, so loud and long that it echoed and re-echoed off the stone walls. He clapped a hand over his mouth but it was too late: the room exploded. At the long tables people pounded the boards and roared so hard that a few of them dropped off the benches and rolled on the floor. At the king's table, the men rocked laughing in their chairs and the ladies turned aside to sputter against their palms. The Chamberlain sat down slowly, his mouth still covered, just as Renard climbed to his feet and raised his cup.

"Gentlemen! Ladies!" he shouted over the din. "A toast to the Lord Chamberlain, *the most eloquent man in all of Longmarch!*"

"The Chamberlain! The Chamberlain!" people called, stomping their feet and raising their cups. The Chamberlain himself sat unmoving in his chair, his face flushed to a color that almost matched the canopy over the king.

Only after long minutes did the laughter and shouts begin to fade. The Chamberlain did not seem interested in speaking again: he frowned at his platter and picked at the remains of his meal. When the noises had settled nearly back to normal, the king pulled his cloak about him and rose to his feet.

The room fell silent at once. The king, his face perhaps not quite as sad as it had been at the beginning of the feast, looked down before he began to speak.

"Good people," he said, "tonight our Lord Chamberlain has spoken great truths. He has reminded us that honor and duty are the measure of a kingdom. No man may ignore this—not even a king. The path we are given is often the hard path, whether we wish it or not."

The king turned briefly to the queen. "As I pondered these things, I thought of Harold. During the years we forged the treaty with Crannocmere he did not leave my side, even in the dark days when it seemed our hopes would fail. And he would remind me that when all is said and done, the hardest path for any kingdom may be the way of peace.

"So I say now, let us choose the hard path once again. Tomorrow, Crannocmere sends a delegation to bring the condolences of their court. We shall receive them in all honor and courtesy. I charge you to greet them as kinsmen and offer them the hospitality of this house. Remember your love for Harold, and all will be well...."

It seemed for a moment that he would speak further, but he looked down again and stepped away from the table. Every person in the hall rose to their feet as the king walked alone to a back corner and out through a doorway. The people returned to their benches and many began to talk and eat, though with little of the noise and fervor they had shown earlier.

Ariel came back to the fireplace where Jessica waited. "That was *so* great," Jessica said. "You were amazing. And funny the way you did it."

"Yeah. The guy was smart, but he was really stuck up. He made it easy for me." Ariel looked over to the doorway in the corner and said, "I think maybe we should follow the king."

"Okay."

They slipped between the tables and out through the door,

which opened into a narrow corridor. The king's footsteps echoed somewhere ahead of them and they hurried to catch up. He took a confusing route from one corridor to another, down some steps and then up a few more, until they arrived at a barred wooden door with a guard standing to one side. The king unlatched the door and pushed it open, and when Jessica and Ariel followed, they stepped outside the castle.

Below them a rocky slope dropped down to a lakeshore, dark and still under an overcast sky. On every side of the lake thick forests slanted up from the water, broken here and there by pinnacles of stone that thrust above the treetops. The king took a narrow path that angled down the slope and ran along the shoreline. After passing the first few trees, the path veered away from the lake, climbing and zigzagging between the dark trunks.

They came to a place where one of the rock pinnacles rose up through a clearing in the forest. In the rubble at the base of the pinnacle, a large stone had been raised upright, with runes and other designs carved into its face. Jessica couldn't read the words but it didn't matter: she knew this was Harold's resting place.

The king walked with heavy steps and dropped down beside the stone, pulling his knees to his face and wrapping his arms around them. He sat there without moving and without a sound.

Ariel perched herself on a rock not far away and motioned for Jessica to join her. Jessica felt awkward—if the king wanted to be alone, were they intruding on his privacy? But she sat and waited, looking out to the lake or watching the mists that drifted through the treetops, and before long Ariel began to play.

The melody was beautiful, slow and a little solemn and a little lonely. It seemed to speak of wind and trees and earth and stone, as though Ariel had found the hidden voices in the clearing and woven them into a song. The king seemed to hear it too, in his own way: his arms relaxed and he almost swayed in time with Ariel's rhythm. He lifted his head, his face softening. "A good place," he murmured. "A good place for a man to rest."

He placed a hand against the upright stone and patted it gently, as he might have patted the head of a child. "I've done what you wanted," he said. "In spite of myself. We will keep the peace. No blood vengeance. Do you know how hard that is for me?" He spread his hand against the rock. "But of course you know. You knew me better than anyone, even your mother."

He looked out across the lake, listening again, and shook his head. "You would have been a marvelous king," he said. "Now Longmarch will never know it. I think that saddens me most of all." He sat silent for a time, then rose and straightened his cloak. He walked out of the clearing and down the trail without looking back.

Ariel kept playing and made no move to follow the king. The music still felt beautiful and rather sad, but also oddly comforting. Jessica listened to it echo off the stone and drift with the mists, and she thought she would be happy to stay there as long as Ariel wanted to play. But in a short while the music rose to its last few notes, clear and trailing like the call of a bird, and the melody lost itself in the wind ruffling the branches of the trees.

Jessica sighed. "That was so good. I'm glad you did that for the king."

"Thanks," Ariel said in a quiet tone. "It kind of happened by itself...it's really peaceful here."

"Yeah. While you were playing, I was even feeling like Harold was lucky to be buried here. Does that sound weird?"

"No. I know what you mean."

They were quiet until Jessica said, "Should we move now? Maybe we've been here long enough."

"Sure."

They got up and walked down the slope of the clearing, towards a flat shelf of rock that looked out over the lake. Jessica said, "It was funny, the way he did that."

"Did what?"

"The way the king patted the stone when he talked to Harold. I do the same thing."

"Oh? How?"

They sat down cross-legged on the rock. "Sometimes at night when I'm missing my brother, I'll put my hand on the wall next to his room. I think about the sounds he used to make before he went away. It makes me feel like I could still hear him if I tried hard enough."

"Oh, that's sad. I didn't know about your brother."

"Well...I don't talk about it much."

Jessica surprised herself a bit by telling the story now, a short version anyway. She talked about Brad's composure and his strength, always willing to hear her and make her feel safe from the time she was young. She described his arguments with their father, the small fights leading up to the big fight, when Brad disappeared in the dark without a word to anyone. She told about never hearing from him in two years and how she wished she could speak to him again, even for a minute, because she felt certain she could help him if he only gave her a chance.

She looked at Ariel then; the girl was resting her chin in one hand and watching her closely. "Wow, I didn't see it," she said.

"See...what?"

"The thing with your brother. It's been so hard for you and I didn't see it before."

"Well—well, yeah," Jessica stammered. "Really hard, some-times. Maybe worse now than before."

Ariel brought up her pipes and fingered them briefly. "I

91

want to make some music now that's just for you. I could make you see your brother if you want to."

"What?"

"I mean, not really see him, where he is. Just in your head. You want me to do it? It won't hurt or anything."

Jessica wrinkled her nose. "Well...I suppose so. Okay."

Ariel played, and the first notes were hardly in the air before Jessica's breath caught in her chest.

She was standing beside a noisy stream that rushed and splashed and chattered over angular granite rocks. She knew the place: she'd seen it on a hike during a family vacation years ago. Spray from the stream chilled her bare legs, a small backpack strained her narrow shoulders, the scent of pine tingled in her nose and left a sharp taste on her tongue. She looked to her right and Brad was there, just a few feet away, reaching down to scoop up snow from a snowbank that had somehow survived into July. Jessica could see spattered mud on his boots and sweat stains on the back of his shirt. He turned to her, holding out the handful of summer snow, and he smiled, grateful to be hiking in the mountains and happy that she could be with him. Jessica blinked because the colors were so bright and he seemed so perfect and alive. She reached out to touch the snow, touch his hand....

The music trailed off and the image slipped away. Jessica found she was shaking and her eyes were wet. She wiped at them as Ariel leaned closer and touched her cheek.

"Jessica, you're crying," she said. "Oh no, did I hurt you?"

Jessica shook her head. "No. No, you didn't."

"That's terrible, I just wanted to make you feel better."

"You did, really. It was beautiful...it's just...I think I was already hurt. It's not your fault." She pressed the heels of her hands against her eyes. "I mean, what if he's dead? What if he died somewhere and nobody knows and I'll never find out? I can't even let myself think about it—" She rubbed a sleeve across her face and wiped her hands on her jeans. "This is dumb. I never cry like this."

Ariel hugged her then, almost fiercely. "I never, ever want to hurt you or make you feel bad. You understand? I'm always going to help you. I'll always help you any way I can do it, I promise."

Jessica hugged her back, surprised. "Okay, I understand."

"And I want to help you find your brother. I can look for him sometimes. I can go places that—that are hard to get to. Where other people can't go. I'll do everything I can do."

"That's great. That's so wonderful," Jessica said. "And I want to help you too, you know. I mean, I don't know how, but whatever I can. I promise."

Ariel hugged her again. "You are so amazing. You're the best friend in the whole world." Jessica didn't know how to answer that, but she felt a sudden happiness, hearing the words. And she realized she hadn't felt that way in a very long time.

Chapter 6

The Mansion by the Marsh

THE NEXT DAY, a warm and windy Saturday, Jessica and Mitch rode their bikes to the McNultys' house again. They all sat on folding chairs near the blackboard in the library while Jessica described her trip with Ariel. She took time to cover all the details, though she decided not to mention the crying at the end (it wasn't important, really, and in any case she figured boys rarely understood that sort of thing).

Mr. McNulty scratched at his chin as he leaned back in his chair; he hadn't shaved that day and the *scritching* of his thumbnail sounded unusually loud. "Maybe we're starting to see a pattern," he said.

"Yeah. Ariel goes around helping people," Mitch said. "She does good deeds."

"Like a boy scout, you mean?"

"Or an angel, maybe,"

Jessica shook her head. "She's not an angel. She really is a girl. Even with all the stuff I don't understand, I'm sure about that."

"Okay, she's a girl," said Mitch, "and she has these special powers, and she tries to help people."

"Right."

"And she does it because Mr. Peabody asks her to."

"Right."

"And we still don't know who he is. Or who she is, really. Or how she can possibly do what she does."

Jessica sighed. "Right." She knew the situation had gotten frustrating for Mitch, a puzzle with too many pieces missing. She wished she had more to offer.

Mitch spoke to Mr. McNulty. "Remember when you told us about *The Tempest*, that Shakespeare play? You said someone in the play is like a sorcerer."

"Yep, the main character, Prospero."

"And the 'Ariel' in the play is his servant?"

"Right. Seems that Prospero put a spell on Ariel sometime in the past, and Ariel has to do whatever he asks. You thinking this Mr. Peabody might be another Prospero?"

"Could be. Suppose, like, he did a spell on Jessie's Ariel, and he's taking advantage of her for some kind of plot."

"Well...I don't know about that," Jessica said. "Ariel doesn't act like anyone's controlling her. She said she does jobs for Mr. Peabody because he helped her, somehow. She even said he rescued her, but she didn't explain it."

"Uh-huh, I heard that," Mitch said. "And I'd like to know, how could someone like Ariel ever need rescuing?"

"Yeah. Good point."

"So, suppose Mr. Peabody tricked her? Or maybe the spell made Ariel *believe* he rescued her. So now she's grateful and wants to help him. First, he gives her some jobs she enjoys, but later he'll have her steal things or mess with his enemies. You see?"

Mr. McNulty was scratching his chin again. "Seems like we might be gettin' wild with the speculating."

"Yeah—yeah, maybe," Mitch said, looking deflated.

"Don't take that wrong: speculating's good. Stay loose, keep the options open. Otherwise we might miss something important. Like, maybe we're not seeing the real point of this thing. If we looked at it from some other angle it might all make sense."

"Oh? Like how?" Jessica asked.

Mr. McNulty took off his glasses and cleaned them. "Well, now—maybe I'm the one who's speculating too much. What really matters, I'd say, is that you've got a good thing going here with your friend. Let's just follow it out and see what else we learn."

"All right," Jessica said, though she wasn't quite sure what he meant.

"Well, here's one more idea," Mitch said. "Or it's an old idea, I guess. How about asking Ariel to meet me?"

"Meet you? You couldn't even see her," Jessica said.

"Yeah, but what if she could change that somehow?"

"Oh...right. Like play music that would change you, or make her visible."

"Yeah. Then maybe she'd let me ask questions, or I'd see something you didn't." He opened his hands, saying, "It probably won't work, but at least it's *something*."

Jessica was already nodding her head. "Sure, I'll ask. I'll talk to her when she shows up."

"Cool. So that's Tuesday?"

"Yeah—she said four days, so Tuesday morning. If she can do it, I'll come find you."

"One thing to remember," Mr. McNulty said. "Don't push it if you feel like it's not going to work. Like I say, let's not mess up a good thing."

"Got it," Jessica said.

"Good. Then if there's no other business, I suggest we adjourn and start some sandwiches."

．　．　．

97

Jessica had begun to feel that the only interesting times in her life were the hours she spent with Ariel, and she found it increasingly difficult to pay close attention to anything else. But her obligations at home and at school hadn't disappeared, and between one thing and another she'd fallen behind on several of them.

The most pressing task was a project for Personal Geography. All the students had been assigned to draw a map of the region they lived in (or, as Mike the teacher put it, "your own personal world"). It was due Tuesday morning and she hadn't started it yet. So, Sunday afternoon she bought a sheet of poster board from a local store and began laying out the streets in her neighborhood and in the valley. She made good progress, but the old roadmap she'd used for reference didn't have enough detail. On Monday in the school library she used a computer to search for aerial photos and worked on the project intensively all evening.

Tuesday morning, with a great sense of relief, she walked into Personal Geography and pinned her finished poster on the front wall. She sat at her desk and watched other kids as they arrived and pinned up their work, and looking at them she realized, with a kind of slow creeping horror, that she'd done the assignment entirely wrong. Everyone else seemed to understand that "personal world" didn't mean your literal neighborhood. One boy had drawn pictures of the best locations for skateboarding near his home. A girl had pasted together still photos from her favorite movies. Someone had drawn a picture of Los Angeles with sheer cliffs around the edges, as though the world came to an end at the borders, and someone else had laid out a floor plan for the ultimate shopping mall. Jessica's map was the only one that actually had streets.

She spent the period with her ears burning, certain that every snicker in the room meant someone was laughing at her. When Mike the teacher commented on the maps, he said hers showed "impressive accuracy;" but somewhere behind her Jessica heard a whisper about "dumb local kids."

By the time the period ended she felt more anxious than ever for Ariel to show up. She kept watch in her other classes, expecting the girl to climb through a window again or pop up in the hallway between periods. But the morning passed with no sign of her.

At the lunch bell, Jessica walked to the same bench where she'd been sitting when Ariel last appeared. A chill breeze blew through the quad, the first cool wind of autumn, scattering bits of trash and sending some of the students to eat indoors. She sat and chewed her food deliberately, her eyes raised the whole time. When she swallowed her last bite of apple she was still alone.

Leaving the quad, she crushed her empty lunch bag and tossed it into a recycling bin. "The day can't really get worse," she muttered. "That's something, anyway."

She walked to the exercise area and found Mitch at an outdoor basketball court. He seemed to be running a drill that required shooting the ball, rebounding, dribbling, then shooting again, all without slowing his pace. When he noticed her, Jessica said, "You can keep playing. She didn't show."

"Oh, too bad," he said, grunting as he put up a shot. The ball caromed off the backboard and he ran outside the court to get it.

"Yeah. She's flaky sometimes. Or most of the time."

"Uh-huh," Mitch said as he returned.

"But I really wanted to see her today. It's frustrating."

"Uh-huh." Mitch put in a layup, then dribbled to the outside again. "It's funny that imaginary friends—" he said as he shot, "—don't always do what you want them to."

"Yeah." She wrinkled her nose as the words sank in. "Umm —what was that?"

"Huh? What?" Mitch dribbled again, then tossed up another shot that bounced high off the rim.

"You said 'imaginary friend.' Why'd you say that?"

Mitch caught the ball on the bounce and bent over with a hand on his knee, catching his breath; it looked as though he didn't want to respond. Jessica felt her stomach muscles tighten. "Wait a minute," she said, "did *he* say it? Did Mr. McNulty say it?"

Mitch straightened with a grimace. "Oops," he said.

"Oops? What do you mean, oops?"

"I mean, I goofed up. It was dumb to...okay, he said it, but it's not like it sounds. He was just kind of thinking out loud. He does that a lot."

Jessica glared at him. "Tell me *exactly* what he said."

Mitch looked up and sighed. "It's like this. We were talking on the phone last night. He said he thought you were really special, and I asked why. He said he knew you'd had big problems, in your family and stuff, and a lot of people in your place would be totally messed up. Then he said, *If she gets help from an imaginary friend, I'm not gonna argue. Sometimes I wish I had one myself.*"

Jessica's next breath got stuck in her chest—she felt as though someone had kicked her. Mitch kept talking, rushing to get the words out. "Like I said, it's not the way it sounds—he didn't mean Ariel's not real. Not like he's sure about it. He plays around with different ideas all the time and he looks for ones that make the most sense. But it's not like he's made up his mind."

Jessica shook her head; a pulse beating hard under her jaw was making her dizzy. "So I'm crazy, is that it? I've told him everything and now he thinks I'm nuts?"

"No, it's not like—"

"What do you *mean* it's not like that? He said it happened in my head. What *else* is it supposed to mean?"

"No, I'm not saying it right...okay, look, here's what he's thinking. The first job you did with Ariel, there was a married couple that was fighting and maybe splitting up. They were kind of like your own parents, right? And you helped them, right?"

"Yeah, maybe."

"Then you saw that king whose son got killed—he lost his son, like you lost your brother. Ariel helped those people and it seemed like she made you feel better too."

"Okay. So?"

"So Mr. McNulty's thinking, maybe that's the point. If Ariel helps you with problems, then it's a good thing and he doesn't care if it's totally real. Get it? He just thinks it doesn't matter." Jessica blinked and dropped her eyes because she couldn't look at him anymore. Mitch said, "I'm still not saying it right."

Jessica's hands had already balled up; she squeezed them tighter. "And you believe him?"

"What?"

"You heard me. You agree with him?"

"No! I always believe you, you know that." He dribbled twice and took a shot. "There's a funny thing, though."

"What?"

He chased down the ball and dribbled again. "I reminded Mr. McNulty you were gonna ask Ariel to meet me today. He said there's probably no way for Ariel to do that. He said don't be surprised if she doesn't show up." He took another shot and ran for the rebound. "See? It's funny."

Jessica watched him miss one more shot, then turned without speaking and walked away. Mitch called after her but she didn't hear what he said.

In her classes that afternoon Jessica did her best to act normally, but it wasn't easy. Sometimes without thinking she would start rocking her feet on the floor or drumming her knuckles on the desktops. When she tried to take notes her handwriting got jagged and the pen kept ripping the paper. She took long breaths to relax and found that it helped, at least a bit, but nothing could alter the fact that she was absolutely seething with anger.

After fifth period, she stalked to her locker, talking to herself the whole time. "How could he say that?" she said under her breath. "How could he *think* that? I trusted them. I *trusted* them. I told them *everything*. It's not fair. They can't *do* that to me."

When sixth period ended her school day was over. On the way back to the locker she muttered, "I should've kept my mouth shut. I should've known better. No one would believe a story like that. If I'd kept quiet, no one could hurt me." She dropped off some books and headed to the front of the school. The bus was parked off to the right but she wasn't taking the bus; she turned to the left and started walking home.

The cool breezes had strengthened during the afternoon and she zipped up her jacket as she walked. "It doesn't matter what he thinks," she muttered, talking about Mr. McNulty. "Why should I care? It doesn't matter what either of them thinks. Who cares what stupid ideas they have? *It doesn't matter.*"

But that was the problem: for reasons she couldn't see, it *did* matter. She'd spent hours turning it inside out and flipping it around in her head but nothing had changed. Every time she pictured Mr. McNulty frowning and shaking his head and saying *imaginary friend,* she felt another twist in her gut. She wanted to believe it didn't make a difference, but it did. And she couldn't make it stop.

By the time she reached the house her hair felt gritty and the wind had made her nose run. She opened the door with her key and locked it from the inside. When she turned around she almost bumped into Ariel, who was standing just inside the entryway.

"Hi there!" she said. "Ready to go?"

Jessica threw up her arms. "What are you *doing* here? And why didn't you show up at school when you were supposed to?"

"I couldn't make it. But I'm all set now. You ready?"

"No, I'm not ready! I can't just run off anytime you feel like showing up!" Jessica stalked through the living room and down the hallway to her bedroom. When she opened the door, Ariel was standing in the middle of the floor.

Jessica rolled her eyes. "Would you cut that out!"

Ariel put a fist on her hip. "Jessica, what's with you? I hardly ever get to see you and you're acting like a big poophead. What's wrong with you?"

Groaning, Jessica dropped down backwards onto her bed and wrapped her arms around her face. "I had a really, really horrible day and I don't want to talk about it and I don't want to see anyone and I don't want to go anywhere. I just want peace and quiet and I want everyone to leave me alone."

"That's dumb," Ariel said. "You can't have any fun if you just lie around." She tugged on Jessica's arm. "Come on, please? It's a quick job this time, and I've got some stuff to tell you but I can't do it now or we'll be late. So please get up and let's go, okay? Please? Please?"

"*All right!*" Jessica said, shaking off her hand. "Just wait a minute." She sat on the edge of the bed, combing back her hair with her fingers and then rubbing the backs of her hands against her eyes. "I needed to ask you," she said, "is there a way you can make someone see you, when you're in-between? Someone else besides me?"

"Nope. I never learned to do that. Why?"

Jessica shook her head. "It figures. Never mind. Just tell me what to do."

Ariel described the picture Jessica had to imagine, and it

seemed rather complex: "a kind of a green pretzel that's stretched out longways and twisted." Jessica wasn't sure she understood but she made the image in her head anyway. She closed her eyes and listened to Ariel's music, and when she opened them again nothing had changed.

Ariel squinted at her, frowning, then said, "Oh, it has to twist to the right, not the left. Sorry!" Jessica sighed and shifted the picture, twisting it the other direction, and knew at once she had it right. When Ariel played the music, she felt herself stretching and twisting like the pretzel until she suddenly snapped back into place.

Jessica opened her eyes and blinked but it didn't help: everything around her was black. "Ariel?" she said.

"Right here," came her voice. "It's dark, huh?"

"Uh, yeah. Where are we?"

"In some woods near a swamp. Here, take my hand." Jessica felt a touch on her fingers and she took hold of it. Ariel began leading and Jessica followed cautiously.

The ground felt squishy under her shoes and the air smelled like damp socks. As her eyes adjusted, she began to see trees around her, tall smooth trees with narrow trunks. From many of the branches strands of moss hung like streamers of dark hair and Jessica had to dodge them as they walked.

"How far do we have to go?" she said, her voice sounding oddly loud.

"Not far. But it's almost dawn, so we need to hurry."

Up ahead a lighter swath cut through the gloom. When they made their way through the last few trees Jessica found that the swath was an old road paved with cobblestones, with tufts of grass sprouting through the cracks. Some yards up the road stood an ancient-looking gate, at least a dozen feet tall. Thick vines had strangled the stone posts, and the barred panels of the gate hung precariously, as though ready to fall off their hinges. Jessica jerked her head towards it and said, "That way?"

"Right."

They squeezed through a gap between two bars and walked out into a broad open space. The road circled around an overgrown area that had once been a landscaped lawn, and on the far side it crossed in front of the largest house Jessica had ever seen. It stood four or five stories tall with leaded glass windows on the first floor and balconies and gables on the higher floors all across the face. Even in the dim light she could see that the house had seen better days: the roof had bare patches where shingles had curled and fallen away, a few of the balconies had nearly collapsed, and ivy had engulfed many of the windows.

"Does anyone live there?" Jessica asked. "It looks deserted."

"Just one person. And she's the one we need to see."

"All right. Let's do it so we can go home."

They cut across the lawn, picking through bushes and skirting the marshy spots, then crossed a paved courtyard and climbed the steps to the porch. The entrance had a double door, with the right-hand door cracked open; Ariel pulled it wider.

They stepped into a vestibule that had once been fit for a mansion. Dark-veined marble paved the floor, and across from the doors a double staircase curved upward with railings carved of oak and carpeting patterned with threads of gold. Above them skylights studded a domed ceiling, while down from the center on a long chain hung a brass-armed chandelier, glinting with hundreds of crystals.

It had all been beautiful once. But now it seemed that every surface was warped, or peeling, or blotched with mold, or stained with old rainwater. And there were spuds everywhere.

They padded across the floor like bugs and clambered along the walls like spiders. They clung to candleholders and hung from the chandelier and crawled along the railings and steps of the staircase. A few looked bulbous and potato-shaped like the first one Jessica had seen, but not many; the varieties of shape and size seemed endless. But they were all colored the same shade of moldy gray, and it seemed to Jessica that they had all stopped their movements and turned to stare at the two of them with unblinking eyes.

"Yuck," Jessica said. The sudden revulsion she'd felt at the king's feast had hit her again, even worse this time, almost strong enough to turn her stomach.

"Yeah, I forgot to tell you," Ariel said quietly. "Lotta spuds here."

"Can you make them go away?"

"Nope. Too many in the house. We'll just have to be careful."

She led the way to a pair of doors in the left wall; the spuds near the doors moved aside when Ariel swung them open.

They entered a grand dining hall with oaken beams crossing above a formal thick-legged table, long enough for fifty guests. Every part of the room was draped in cobwebs and layered with dust, and the spuds seemed even thicker here than in the vestibule, climbing across the beams and crawling two or three deep around the floors.

Ariel walked ahead with calm deliberate steps and Jessica followed, trying to ignore her queasiness. The spuds squirmed away from their feet, some of them hissing or glaring, clearly unhappy with the intrusion.

"What are they doing here?" Jessica whispered.

"Not sure," Ariel said. "But some bad things happened here, a long time ago. Maybe they hang around 'cause they can still feel it. Something like that."

As they passed the length of the table Jessica saw place settings at every chair, as though someone had prepared the table for a banquet that never took place. Under the dust every item seemed exquisite, jade-colored china and crystal goblets and saltcellars shaped like horses and dragons. Even the silver-ware looked remarkable, in Jessica's eyes: the handles on every piece were miniature sculptures, silver tangles of climbing roses with a sort of family crest in the center, inlaid with enamels and studded with tiny gems.

Mitch ought to see some of this stuff, she thought. *Then he'd know I'm not imagining things.*

They reached the end of the room without difficulty, passing into a short corridor that led to a kitchen surprisingly small for such a large house. Beyond the kitchen was a room full of cupboards—a pantry, probably—and then through another doorway they came to a narrow stairwell.

Ariel began climbing and Jessica followed. The stairs, made of unfinished wood, had a steep pitch and switched back frequently. Three stories up they came to a landing with two doors, one of them open; Ariel walked through the open door without stopping.

They entered a dark musty space. Blankets hanging over the windows allowed a seeping light along the edges, enough to let Jessica make out the bare walls and the only furniture, a narrow four-poster bed with sheets and rags piled on the mattress. Aside from a few books and crumpled papers on the floor, the room looked empty.

Ariel stopped after they entered and seemed to be waiting. Jessica said, "Is this where we're going? There's no one here."

"Yes there is," Ariel said.

Something on the bed shifted and wheezed. Jessica blinked, realizing that the pile of rags was actually a worn-out robe, and inside the robe was a woman, a small old woman who seemed to be waking up. "Oh, I didn't see," Jessica said. "Is she all right?"

"Not really."

"Is she the caretaker or something?"

"No, she's the owner. The whole place belongs to her."

The woman snorted and coughed, shifting to the edge of the mattress, sitting up as she pulled the tattered robe around her. She looked painfully thin, the flesh on her wrists and hands barely disguising the bones. She spat on the floor and took a harsh breath, rubbing one eye with a shaky hand.

Ariel said, "She stays here all the time. She never sees anyone, and almost never leaves this room, except to get oatmeal or something from the kitchen. She's been like this for years."

"That—that's terrible," Jessica said. "Why would she do that if she owns the whole place?"

"Don't know. Some awful things happened here and they were mostly her fault. Now she's alone, and she lives this way because she wants to. That's all I know for sure."

The faint light in the room had brightened somewhat. The old woman turned towards the windows, then eased herself up from the bed.

"It's time," Ariel said. She stepped to one side and got her pipes ready. With a few shuffling steps the woman approached the window, then pulled the blanket aside and peered out.

Through the narrow strip of glass Jessica could see a misted landscape, thick with trees, rolling in the distance to a dark line of mountains. Above them the sky shown like opal, long clouds streaking the high air with orange and red. The woman blinked and leaned forward, placing her free hand against the glass. Before she took her next breath there came a flare of fire on the horizon, the first bright pearl of the sun.

Ariel began to play, a simple tune that quickly grew powerful, rising and rising along with the dawn. Gazing out at the first light the woman seemed to change: her eyes widened, the harsh edges of her wrinkles softened, the arch of her back settled and relaxed. The golden light caught the fine hairs on her head and set them glowing. She leaned closer to the window, her mouth slackened from surprise or a kind of delight.

She held herself there, caught up somehow by the music and the sunlight; then for no reason that Jessica could see the moment ended. The woman pressed her eyes closed and turned her head, scowling as though she'd tasted something bitter. She let the blanket fall and shuffled back to the bed, sitting with a grunt and rubbing her forehead with one hand.

Ariel stopped playing and slung her pipes back over her shoulder. Jessica said, "What, are you finished?"

"Uh-huh."

"You're kidding."

"Nope."

"It took like ten seconds."

Ariel shrugged. "That was the job. It's the only time of the day when she lets anything inside. I tried to give her something but I guess she didn't want it."

"Well...did it help?"

"I don't know."

Jessica blew out some air. "We came all that way so you could play for no reason? That's silly. It's not worth the trouble."

Ariel shrugged again. "I don't know how you tell what's worth it and what isn't."

"Well—whatever. If it's done, fine. Let's get out of here and go home."

As she followed Ariel down the narrow stairs Jessica gave no more thought to the woman in the room, or to anything Ariel had done or hadn't done. Instead, she found herself thinking about the table in the dining hall.

She had never seen anything as perfect as the ornaments and the place settings on that table. She felt certain Mitch had never seen anything like them, and it might even be true for

Mr. McNulty as well. It occurred to her again that if they could only see some of it, even a single piece, they'd almost *have* to believe she'd been telling the truth.

So why not pick up one of the pieces—even just a spoon—and bring it home to show to them?

Bad idea, she thought. *Stealing is wrong. I'm not turning into a thief.*

Of course not...but maybe she didn't have to steal it. She could *borrow* a piece of silverware. She would only need it for a few days. After the guys had seen it, she could ask Ariel to bring her back to return it.

And who would miss it? The table hadn't been touched for years. The old woman hardly left her room. She wouldn't notice and she wouldn't care.

When you looked at it that way, was it even a big deal? The problem would be solved and no one would get hurt.

No, it's crazy, and it's still wrong, she thought. *Just forget about it. It's not going to happen.*

At the bottom of the stairs they crossed through the pantry and back into the small kitchen. A few more steps took them down the short corridor, returning to the dining hall, with the cobwebs and the spuds and the long, long table.

Passing beside the chair backs Jessica glanced at the sculpted silverware one last time. As she did an image popped into her head: Mr. McNulty shaking his head and muttering *imaginary friend*. And then Mitch shooting a basket and saying *See? It's funny.* She felt her neck grow hot as the anger flared up all over again.

She was walking about a half-step behind Ariel. Without breaking stride, she raised one hand and let it drift above the tabletop. When she neared the next place setting she let her hand fall and took hold of a spoon. It was heavier than she expected but she lifted it and slipped it into her pocket. She left a swirl of dust but didn't make a sound.

It was easy.

Her heart had been thudding fast; she took a long breath and relaxed. They were nearing the end of the table, approaching the vestibule and the front doors. In a moment they'd be outside and Ariel would take her home. Jessica pictured the scene a day from now, when she would tell the story to Mitch and Mr. McNulty. She saw herself casually reaching into her pocket and bringing out the marvelously sculpted spoon. They'd be startled, maybe even embarrassed. They would apologize two or three times for ever doubting her. It's all right, she'd say with a smile, don't feel bad, I know it sounds crazy if you haven't been there....

Something was tugging at her arm. She looked down to see a spud pulling on her wrist, a short creature with long spindly arms. It seemed to have no head, but set in the middle of its chest were a pair of eyes and a nose and a lipless mouth. The eyes looked up at her and blinked.

"You took a spoon," it said in a thin voice.

"What? Hey!" Jessica said, trying to pull her hand away. "What are you talking about? Let go!"

Ariel had stopped and turned around. "What's the matter? What's wrong?" she said.

"I saw you," the spud said to Jessica. "You took a spoon."

"I did not. Let go of me, leave me alone!" She managed to break loose, but the spud kept reaching for her wrist and she had to bat its fingers away.

"Jessica, what's he mean?" Ariel said.

"It's nothing. Let's just go."

"I saw you," the spud said again. "You took—"

"Oh, *never mind!*" Jessica said. Turning back to the table she pulled out the spoon and slapped it on the tabletop. As the sharp echoes died she noticed, in a distant sort of way, that aside from her own noises the room had gone silent.

"There, it's fixed," she said, returning to Ariel. "Can we get out of here, please?"

Ariel watched her with an odd expression; she didn't seem shocked or angry, just quizzical. "I don't get it," she said. "Why'd you do that? Where were you taking it?"

Jessica rolled her eyes in frustration. "It was stupid, okay? I'm sorry. Let's just—"

Something struck hard on her forehead—she said "Ow!" and took a half-step back, pressing a hand to her head. A clattering sound came from the floor; looking down she saw a small rock bouncing to a stop. She couldn't quite believe it, but one of the spuds must have thrown it at her. She squeezed her hand harder, and when she took it away her fingers were stained with a spot of blood, shockingly bright and red.

Jessica looked up and met Ariel's eyes. There was something in them she'd never seen there before. It almost looked like fear.

Off to the right, Jessica heard a thin shuddery voice: "She bleeds."

From behind them came a harsh croaking voice: "She's *mortal.*"

From the rafters above them came a low rasping voice: "They're *both* mortal."

Then from every part of the room Jessica heard a new sound, a kind of rising hiss, as though a hundred different creatures were drawing a long breath all at the same time.

Ariel spun on one foot and blew a blast on her pipes, so loud that Jessica squinted and gritted her teeth. All around them, the spuds cringed and covered their ears and a few rolled on the floor in pain, but not one of them left the room. When Ariel stopped spinning she grabbed Jessica's hand and yelled "*Run!*"

She didn't need any other encouragement. They sprinted from the room into the vestibule, where most of the spuds also seemed dazed. Behind them they heard a wild mix of yelping and snarling that quickly rose to a long angry howl.

They shoved out through the front door and jumped down the porch steps, running across the courtyard to the lawn. Looking back Jessica said, "Will they stay inside—"

Both front doors flew open and the spuds burst out in a flood, rolling, running, clawing over each other and screaming like animals on a hunt. Jessica looked away and tried to run faster.

"How do we get out of here?" she huffed.

"You have to move a certain way...when I play," Ariel panted. "I can't show you while we're running."

"Let's not stop," Jessica said.

"No. We'd better go faster."

When they reached the gate, they could hear trampling behind them. They slipped through the gap and ran down the road just as the first spuds slammed against the iron bars. Jessica looked over her shoulder and saw the creatures piling up behind the gate. The spuds closest to the bars had been pressed so tightly they couldn't move and only a few small ones had managed to squirm through the gap.

"It's stopping them," she said.

"Good," Ariel said. "Keep running."

"Right," Jessica said. Then a few strides later, "How far should we get before—"

A great grinding crash of broken metal. Jessica looked back to see that the gates had collapsed and the spuds were pouring through, the faster ones trampling the slower ones if they didn't move aside.

"Ariel," Jessica said, "do you have any other ideas...."

But Ariel had stopped running. She slowed to a walk, then came to a halt and stood in the road with her head hanging.

Jessica stopped with her, panting. "What's the matter? What are you doing?"

Ariel shook her head and said, "Nothing." Then a moment later: "Mr. Peabody is coming."

"Oh," Jessica said, looking back at the spuds. "Is that good?"

Ariel shook her head again. "Maybe." She looked up with a pained expression. "Jessica, I think you'd better cover your eyes."

"Why should I cover—" she said, and then it happened.

Just behind them something enormous ripped into the world. In a brief blurred moment Jessica saw blazing fires and beating wings and eyes—too many wings and too many eyes—before a flood of light and the noise from the thing dropped on her like a crashing wave. She glimpsed the spuds shrieking and scattering like leaves in a gale as she fell groaning to the ground and covered her head with her arms.

Beneath her the roadway shuddered from the presence of the thing and the thundering, shattering sounds that came from it, and she wanted nothing else but to crawl into a hole and hide. But she could tell that Ariel was still beside her and, unbelievably, still standing. And she seemed to be *talking* to the thing, talking in a mournful voice like a child in trouble: "....no, sir...I know...I'm sorry...she was helping me, she helped me a lot...I'm really sorry...." And the voice of the thing kept pounding like boulders crashing down a waterfall, rattling Jessica's teeth and making her muscles jump and twitch.

She could not have said how long it lasted but it ended all at once: the noises went silent and the light went out. Jessica took short shaky breaths and lay without moving. She heard a voice above her: "Young woman...would you—rise, please?"

Jessica shifted an arm so she could look up, then gradually gathered her legs under her and sat back. A man stood in front of her, or something that looked like a man. From the shoulders down a dark cloak covered him, completely hiding any arms or legs. He had a large hooked nose and thick hair that swept backwards all around his face. Almost like a hawk's face, Jessica thought; a hawk or an eagle.

"You are...Jessica?" he said. He didn't sound angry to her but she couldn't actually read the emotions in his voice.

"Y-yes," she stuttered as she stood up. Under her feet the stones of the roadway kept trembling and along the man's outline the light seemed slightly disturbed, making her wonder if the image in front of her was entirely real.

The man's eyes stared dark and unblinking. "You have journeyed...with Ariel?"

"Yes—yes, sir," she said, still shaky. "I'm s-sorry for the trouble...thank you for doing what you did."

"You have that...capacity?" he said. "You have joined in her tasks?"

Jessica glanced at Ariel—the girl was still hanging her head, a pained expression on her face. "I g-guess so," Jessica said. "Is there a problem? I thought everything was going okay. Until today."

The man didn't react. "This was not...anticipated," he said. "It was not expected."

Ariel lifted her head then, looking as though she was close to tears. "I'm so sorry, Jessica," she said. "I didn't tell him about you. I didn't tell him you were doing jobs with me. It's all my fault."

"Well—no it's not," Jessica said. "I mean, you didn't do anything bad, right?"

"This was not expected," the man said. "We must go."

"Jessica, I'm sorry," Ariel said. "You've been so great. It was all wonderful."

"What—what do you mean?" Jessica said. "Where are you going? You'll come back to see me, right?"

"We must go," the man said.

Ariel touched Jessica lightly on the arm, then stepped away.

"A promise is a promise," she said, almost whispering. "Remember that."

"Well, wait," Jessica said, "I don't under*staaaaaaaaaaa*...." Though the man had barely nodded his head she suddenly felt herself hurtle backwards into the dark, faster and wilder than any traveling she had done with Ariel.

And then she stood in the middle of her own room with her head spinning. The bed was still rumpled where she'd lain down; it looked as though she'd been gone about fifteen minutes.

She stumbled to the bathroom in the hallway, leaning on the walls for support, and threw up in the toilet. She washed off her mouth and came back to the room, crawling into bed with her clothes on. She was still shaking when she fell asleep.

Chapter 7

Calling Through the Dark

JESSICA CRACKED her eyelids the next morning when the walls in her room turned gray from the sunrise. She blinked and stretched, half-awake and slightly confused, until she noticed she was wearing clothes instead of pajamas. Then she groaned as the memories returned in a single horrible rush.

"No, that's not right," she said, gripping the bedcovers. "It couldn't happen like that." But she moved a hand to her head and touched a sore spot near the hairline. She felt a small lump, just where the spud hit her with a rock.

At breakfast Jessica ate slowly, finishing only a few mouthfuls of cereal. Her mother asked if she felt all right; Jessica nodded and mumbled a few words. When she got on the bus, she sat several seats away from Mitch. He seemed to understand it wasn't a good day to talk.

At school the morning classes passed in a droning blur. She sat numb and silent at her desk while her mind replayed yesterday's events over and over, as though a part of her brain believed the whole thing would make sense if she could just relive it often enough. But as the hours wore on she knew it wasn't working. She didn't feel any closer to understanding what had happened, she just felt empty and tired.

But she saw one thing clearly enough: all at once, everything had gone completely wrong. If it was bad for Jessica then it certainly must be worse for Ariel. Jessica couldn't decide whether the person who appeared to them (she fought off a surge of fear when she recalled the moment) had actually been angry (whatever that meant for him), or only startled or disturbed that Ariel hadn't told him she'd found a friend. One way or another Ariel seemed to be saying, at the end, that Jessica would never see her again.

Which meant that after all the remarkable things that had happened in the last few weeks, Jessica had nothing to show for it. Except for the lump on her head.

In the middle of the afternoon as she walked along a hallway, Jessica began talking to herself again. "It wasn't fair," she muttered. "I didn't know what was going on, I didn't know *anything*. Of course I make mistakes when it's like that. Someone should have told me the rules. It's not *fair*."

Even while she made the complaint, she had a feeling it wasn't quite true. She remembered Ariel telling her not to touch anything while they were in-between, when they hid the keys from the married couple. At the mansion she'd said they should be especially careful around the spuds. She didn't explain either of those things—like she rarely explained anything—but maybe that should have been enough. Maybe that was all Jessica really needed to know.

The next day, Thursday, the weather turned windy and warmer. In Biology class Ms. Starchild began the period by playing harp music on her CD player. Under the gliding notes Jessica whispered, "It's not my fault. Mitch got me angry. Mr. McNulty shouldn't have said those things. They got me all messed up. Everything would be okay if they hadn't made me mad."

She felt better when she said this, but she knew again it was only partly true. Whatever Mitch and Mr. McNulty had said about her, they weren't at the mansion when everything went wrong. And they didn't tell Jessica to ignore Ariel's warnings. And they didn't ask her to pick up the spoon.

On Friday, the weather turned chilly again. Students came to school bundled in jackets and sweaters, and when Jessica walked to the lunch area only a few other people were sitting outdoors. She sat on her usual bench anyway and started to eat.

Halfway through the sandwich she stopped chewing and sat for a time with her hands in her lap, staring at the ground. Then she looked up and sighed.

"I messed up," she murmured. "I blew it. Just me. I was the luckiest kid in the world, and I totally blew it."

This time she didn't hear any objections in her head. So this time, maybe, she'd gotten it mostly right.

Nothing very interesting happened over the weekend. On Monday Jessica went back to school and nothing very interesting happened there either.

The days settled back into their old routine. In the daytime Jessica went to classes and kept quiet. At night she did schoolwork and watched television. She went to bed at pretty much the same time and got up at pretty much the same time every day. She talked to her mother occasionally but not about anything important. She never talked to Mitch, and she avoided places where she might run into him, sometimes getting a ride from her mother in the morning and walking home in the afternoon so she wouldn't have to take the bus.

Weeks went by without any real changes, except that the days were getting shorter and cooler. Jessica hadn't forgotten any of the things she'd done with Ariel, but the images began to blur around the edges, mingling with memories of other things she'd done, and with scenes she'd seen in movies or read in books, and with ideas she'd only thought about. She had noticed before that, given enough time, she couldn't always tell the difference between her memories and imaginings. Thinking about this one day, she even wondered if Mr. McNulty might have been right: it had all happened in her head, it was a fantasy she needed for a while and now it was gone. She tossed the idea away—it was an idle thought, not to be taken seriously. But as the days plodded one after the other, she found it easier and easier to think it almost made sense.

And sometimes in her room in the quiet of the night she would wonder: if Ariel had been a tool for helping her deal with losing her brother, what was she going to do now?

In an odd way she felt almost glad, during that time, to be a student at Esterhaus, since she could depend on the school to keep creating new distractions. One Wednesday morning as she arrived she saw, stretched over the entrance, a broad blue banner with the words "ALWAYS RISING HIGHER." Coming closer she could see that the letters in the banner had been formed from collages of student photos. Two young women wearing orange vests and many colorful slap bracelets were greeting people as they approached the gate.

One of them spoke to Jessica: "Welcome, Esterhauser! Here's your first spirit words!" She held out a yellow button with a pin on the back—the button said GIVE YOURSELF A HUG. A container in front of her was packed with other pins in a rainbow of colors, sizes, and slogans.

"What's this for?" Jessica said, taking the button.

"It's our first annual Aspiration Day!" The girl's smile was unnaturally bright. "You didn't forget, did you?"

"Oh," Jessica said, thinking about some recent announcements that she hadn't paid attention to. "Maybe I did."

"Well, get ready to rise! Today we pump up our potential and elevate our journey. We're all going to the next level!"

"Oh," Jessica said.

"Have a super day, Esterhauser! Time to shine!" Her smile got even wider.

"Right," Jessica said, walking away and stuffing the button in a side pocket of her jeans.

She hoped that might be the last she'd hear about Aspiration Day; the hope died quickly. The inside of the school had been transformed overnight. Banners festooned the hallways and staircases and railings, all of them blazing with colorful, positive-sounding slogans. Students in orange vests waited at corners with buckets of pins and buttons, and kids were already competing to see how many they could attach to their jackets and caps and pants and shoes. Jessica, for her part, tried to slip through the hallways as quickly as possible, sticking buttons in her pockets when she couldn't avoid them.

The morning classes brought no relief. Each period was interrupted with announcements on the intercom, with quick essays on the topic "How I Rise Every Day" and election guidelines for the Spirit King and Queen. Jessica sat through it all with her head in her hands, and sometimes with her hands over her ears.

Then late in the morning, everything changed.

In fourth period, Jessica's English class, three students performed a skit about a boy at a public school who was doing poorly and getting bad grades. The boy felt upset about this until his friends cheered him up, explaining that it's okay if your IQ is low as long as your SQ is high ("SQ" was short for "Smile Quotient"). Jessica watched the action with her head on one fist, only half awake.

As the skit neared its end the students' voices faded to silence, though Jessica could still see their lips moving. In the odd stillness she heard another sound: a voice, a long drawn-out call, quiet as a whisper: "...*jjjjjeeeeeessssssssssiiiiiiiiiiiiccc-caaaaaaaa....*"

She jerked her head up—faint as it was, it sounded like Ariel. But the voice felt twisted and strained, as though warped by a great effort or by passing across a huge distance. Anyway Ariel was nowhere in sight and no one else in the room had reacted.

The call came again. It began in a whisper, growing louder in stages until it rang in her head like a fire bell.

" ... jjjjjjjjjjjJJJJJEEEEEEEEESSSSSSSSSSSSSSSIIIIIIIIIIIIICCCCC-CCAAAAAAAAAAAaaaaaaaaaa...."

Jessica's whole body trembled as she struggled to take a breath. It was Ariel's voice without a doubt, but there was sorrow in the tone, and fear, and a terrible sense of loss; a cry from some dark place, with no light and no way out. Jessica had never heard anyone sound so grieved and abandoned. Her muscles had drawn tight and she sat with her hands clenched, looking to each side as though something might jump at her from a corner of the room.

Nothing else happened. She heard only ordinary noises, shuffling feet and whispered gossip. The students ended their skit and a few people applauded, and the teacher spoke for a while about nothing in particular until the lunch bell rang. People got up from their chairs and talked among themselves and moved to the doors, the last stragglers making their way out while Jessica sat unmoving at her desk.

She gathered her books and pushed herself up on weak legs. In a kind of daze, she walked to her locker and picked up her bag and went to the lunch area, sitting in some random spot, and started to eat, hardly tasting the food. She finished only half the sandwich before throwing the lunch away. She stalked back to the hallway near her last classroom—there was no other place to go—and paced the hall with a dozen thoughts crisscrossing in her head.

"She's in trouble," she muttered, "and it's *big* trouble." She understood that much. Ariel had called out but hadn't been able to come to her—how could that happen? She'd never had a problem with traveling before, not that Jessica had seen.

Was she hurt? Maybe she'd been injured so badly she couldn't travel. Maybe she couldn't even play her pipes.

Or was there another way to get stuck? Could someone have trapped her on purpose, like the spuds? And there might be worse things than spuds out there. "I've got to *do* something," Jessica said.

But what could she do? She didn't know where Ariel was, and it wouldn't make any difference if she'd known since she couldn't travel without her. Jessica started to say *It's not fair* but cut it off. "That won't help, I've got to think of something."

She neared the doors at the end of the corridor; outside was an open stairwell draped with a banner—EVERY DAY IS YOUR DAY!—and beyond that the small lawn where Jessica had talked with Ariel the day she came to Esterhaus. Jessica walked out and sat on the grass, pressing her hands against her head, scouring her brain for some idea she hadn't already rejected.

"It can't be just me," she said. "Someone else has to help, like Mr. Peabody." That made sense, since he'd rescued them at the mansion. But Ariel would've thought of that. So why didn't she call him instead of Jessica?

A worse thought: what if Mr. Peabody was the problem, the reason Ariel needed help?

Jessica groaned. "This is useless. *I'm* useless. What am I supposed to do?" She dug the toe of her shoe into the grass, and when the toe had turned thoroughly green a new idea popped in her head. She pushed it aside, but after wrinkling her nose she brought it back and looked closer.

It was crazy, of course. More than that it didn't seem safe.

But could it work?

She thought back to Ariel's call, trying to recollect every detail. To her surprise it came back quickly and clearly, as though it were still echoing somewhere inside her. She could hear the long extended tones in Ariel's voice and the shorter, quieter notes that followed them, and the low rumblings that vibrated underneath, like plucked strings on a bass cello. Despite their strangeness the sounds rolled easily through her head. None of them seemed completely foreign; none seemed impossible to recreate.

It might work. But it probably wasn't safe.

She was still thinking when the bell rang for fifth period. She kept thinking through the afternoon classes, waiting for a better idea to pop up unexpectedly. Nothing had changed by the time the last bell rang. At her locker she stood with the door open, staring sightlessly at the clutter of books and papers as she made a decision. She shut the locker door and walked to the front gate.

Outside she found Mitch standing near some of the local kids, playing a handheld video game while he waited for the bus. He raised his head as Jessica walked up. "Mitch, could we talk?" she said.

He blinked in surprise. "Uh, sure. What do—what's up?"

"Well, it's...something's happened. Something's wrong."

"Oh, yeah?"

"It's Ariel. I heard her calling today. I couldn't see her, just heard her voice. She sounded terrible, like she was scared or trapped. I've got to try to help her. But I wanted to talk to you first, so...so you'll know. Like, in case anything goes wrong."

His eyes widened. "Oh, seriously? So, tell me about it."

The bus had pulled up and they kept quiet while they got on board and took a seat by themselves. As the bus rolled Jessica described her last trip with Ariel: the marsh, the gate, the mansion, the spuds, and the old woman in the bare room. She told about picking up the spoon (she stammered through that part but didn't hold back)—then came the flight down the road, the appearing of the thing that became Mr. Peabody, and the parting words from Ariel.

Mitch was grimacing and shaking his head. "Wow," he said. "Whoa."

"Yeah. And after that I didn't see her for weeks. Nothing until I heard her today." She gave him a narrow look. "So, do you believe all that or not? Just tell me, okay?"

"Sure, I believe you. Always. Like I said."

"Uh-huh. What happened when we talked on the basketball court?"

He shrugged. "I forgot for a while."

"You *forgot*?" She bumped him with her elbow. "How could you *forget*? You made me mad! Right before I went off with Ariel!"

He elbowed her back. "So? It's not my fault, you dummy."

She elbowed him again. "Yes it is, and you're the dummy."

He gave her one more. "No, it's you. I'm always trying to believe you, but you keep telling these crazy stories. I never see Ariel—I never see *anything*. I never even get to go *with* you. What am I supposed to think?"

Jessica was ready with another comeback but she let it go. She looked out the window and sighed. "Yeah...I know. It's been really weird. And it's hard, when you don't see it."

"Nah, not that much," he said. "It's been lots harder for you than me. I mean, I know I messed up. I should have trusted you more."

"Yeah, well...I shouldn't get mad so fast, either. That messes me up even worse."

The bus braked at the stop near their street; they got out and crossed the road with other kids from their neighborhood. The breezes were rising again, the dry northerly gusts that people called the Santa Ana Winds. They stirred dry leaves into eddies on the asphalt and rattled branches in the oak tree at the corner. Mitch and Jessica waited near the tree until the other kids were out of earshot.

"So now what?" Mitch said.

Jessica hesitated, chewing her lip. "Well...I'm going to try something. I'm gonna try to call Mr. Peabody."

Mitch stared at her. "No. Seriously? Can you do that?"

"Umm...maybe."

"You think it's dangerous?"

"I'm not sure. But I know I can't reach Ariel—I don't know how I know that, but I know it. So it's the only way I might find her or find out what's happened."

Mitch nodded. "Okay, before you try, could we do one thing? Could we talk to Mr. McNulty?"

Jessica made a sour face. "Why would I do that?"

"Because he should know about this—he'd want to know. He might be able to help."

"He can't help, he thinks I'm crazy."

"No, he doesn't, really."

"Look, I know you like him," she said, "and that's fine. And if he wants to believe it's all in my head that's fine too. I don't care." This wasn't exactly true but she let it pass. "But I'm not going to see him now, I'll just end up getting mad again."

Mitch wasn't giving up. "But I can tell he feels bad about what happened. *Really* bad."

"Fine, whatever. Anyway, I can't wait around, I gotta do this."

"Okay, I'll call him right now," Mitch said, "and maybe my mom can drive us over—she's going to the store anyway." Jessica glared at him but he didn't seem to notice. "Just wait ten minutes," he said. "Please?"

She blew out some air. "All right, ten minutes. After that forget it."

"Cool." He ran off to his house before she could say anything else.

Jessica went to her own home and sat in the living room, watching the clock. She wasn't happy she'd agreed to wait and a part of her hoped that time would run out before she heard from Mitch. But she also knew that would be disappointing, since he'd made her wonder what Mr. McNulty would have to say. In any event the phone rang after six and a half minutes.

"He'll see us," Mitch said on the phone, "and my mom's gonna drive. We can meet you out front."

Jessica turned on a few lights in case she didn't return before dark, then pulled on her padded orange jacket and locked the front door. She reached the sidewalk as Mitch and his mother pulled up at the curb.

They got out of the car beside the McNultys' mailbox. The winds felt stronger here and Jessica zipped her jacket to keep the flaps from whipping around. They found Mr. McNulty and Katie waiting on the front porch; Katie seemed pleased to see them and she chatted for a while, and Jessica answered her questions while glancing now and then at Mr. McNulty. He wore a bulky sweater over a long-sleeve shirt, and she noticed that the shirt collar seemed worn and discolored. He stood rather awkwardly in the wind and didn't say much.

Gradually they moved indoors. When Mitch shut the door Katie said, "I'll let you three get to work," and walked towards the kitchen. Mr. McNulty nodded and said, "Let's go to the library."

Three chairs waited near the blackboard; no one spoke as they sat down. Jessica could hear tree branches scratching the roof and rattling against the walls of the house. She wasn't sure what Mitch expected but she didn't feel like talking. She clasped her hands in her lap and looked at the floor.

Mitch broke the ice. "So, like I was saying on the phone," he said to Mr. McNulty, "I told Jessie you wanted to get together again."

"Right," Mr. McNulty said.

"And she said okay. And she knows I told you what happened on the day when Ariel didn't show up—"

"Right," he said again, almost sighing as he spoke.

"So—you want me to keep going, or...?"

"No, I'll take it. It's only fair." Mr. McNulty leaned forward with his elbows on his knees and rubbed his hands together, blinking at Jessica through his lenses.

"I'm glad you came today," he said. "Sorry it's been so long since we talked."

"It's all right," Jessica shrugged.

"If you'll bear with me, I'll explain a couple things." He folded his hands. "First off, I need to apologize."

"Oh," Jessica said. "Really?"

"Yes." He smoothed his hair with one hand, though there wasn't much to smooth. "I'm sure you know, I've had a hard time getting a handle on this thing."

"Yeah."

"When you started talking to us, I figured, well, let's keep an open mind. Maybe we'll learn something new. But I also figured that, sooner or later, there'd be a reasonable explanation, something that didn't turn the world inside out."

He scratched his nose, looking uncomfortable. "So I looked at possibilities. One of them was, it's all happening in your head, some part of your head. You're not crazy, but you invented a magic friend who solves problems. It's a fantasy that meets a need, even if you don't understand the need." He looked at her with raised eyebrows. "I'm being very blunt here. But you see what I'm saying?"

"I think so," Jessica said. "I mean, it's logical."

"Maybe more to the point, it's comfortable. And convenient. A little too convenient." He took off his glasses and wiped them with a handkerchief. "Anyhow, it was a theory. I'd bring it out once in a while to see if it fit. One day when I was thinking about it, I talked to Mitch on the phone." He put his glasses on and pushed them higher. "I did some of my thinking out loud. And you heard about it the next day at school."

"My fault," Mitch said.

He shook his head. "An accident. In any case," he said to Jessica, "I'm sure, at the time, it was a terrible thing to hear."

After a moment, Jessica said, "Yes, you're right." She felt odd saying the words, but they seemed the right thing to say.

Mr. McNulty nodded, watching her, and took a breath. "Well, then. I'm very sorry about that, for your sake. And I'm sorry I wasn't honest when I should have been."

"Oh," Jessica said. "Umm...when was that, exactly?"

"As soon as I had the idea. We'd been partners in this thing; we all had a responsibility to be open and direct. You wouldn't've been thrilled to hear it, but we would've skipped any misunderstandings. And surprises. So, I let you down when I ought to have known better. I apologize."

This wasn't what Jessica expected to hear but she felt relieved anyway. "Thanks," she said, a little flustered. "I mean, don't be hard on yourself. But thanks."

"You're welcome," he said. "Now, here's how I'd like to make amends. I figure it's time to drop that particular theory."

"Oh...yeah?" Jessica said. "How come?"

"The truth is, it doesn't explain things very well. Doesn't really make sense of your stories. Even worse, like I said, it's too convenient—makes it easy to dodge the tough questions. That's not good for you or for me either.

"So I'm starting a new theory. I'll assume, from the beginning, that you've told us the plain truth. It won't be easy and it's not necessarily the final answer. But I believe I need to start there and see where it takes me—where it takes both of us."

He ran a hand across his head and cleared this throat. "I've done a lot of talking. Did I make sense? Did I answer any questions?"

Jessica nodded, and she blinked because her eyes were watering. "Yeah," she said. "Yes, you did. That really helps."

"Well, I'm glad to hear it."

They were both quiet then. Mitch said to Mr. McNulty, "Just so you know, I already apologized. I was quicker."

"Ahh. So, are we all square?"

Jessica took a breath; the tightness in her chest had loosened, maybe for the first time in weeks. Her whole body felt lighter. "Yeah, thanks. It's just right."

"Not a problem."

Mitch said, "Are you ready for the rest of it?"

"Oh? There's more?"

"Afraid so," Jessica said. She told him the story of the trip to the mansion, covering the same ground as she had with Mitch earlier in the day. She went on to tell about the voice she'd heard at school and her fear that Ariel was in serious trouble. Mr. McNulty sat with his arms crossed, and when Jessica finished, he nodded his head and scratched his chin.

"Fascinating," he said.

"Yeah. So, you want to change your mind, about believing me?"

"Nope. It's more interesting this way."

"Here's the last thing," Mitch said. "She's going to try to call Mr. Peabody. Only she's afraid it might be dangerous."

"Ahh. Seems a legitimate concern."

"I'm not even sure it'll work," Jessica said, "but I'll be careful. I'll do it when no one else is around."

Mitch shook his head. "Uh-uh. Not alone."

"Unless I'm mistaken," Mr. McNulty said, "we decided we're all in this together. Or did I miss something?"

Jessica said, "Yeah, but still—"

"No buts," Mitch said. "We believe you now, remember?"

"Exactly," Mr. McNulty said. "If someone's going to take risks, seems like we all ought to take them."

Mitch broke in when Jessica started to speak. "Do you really want to argue about this?"

She closed her mouth and looked at them both. "No, I don't.

Thanks, again, you guys. You're being great."

"Yeah, well, let's see how it goes, before you say that."

Mr. McNulty said, "You'll want to do this right away?"

"Yes. But not here—not indoors, I mean. I was thinking I should be outside, in some quiet place. Like it might work better that way, or be safer. Maybe."

Mr. McNulty considered it. "We've got the yard, o'course, but there's another possibility. Just up in the hills out back there's a place not many people know about. Plenty of room, but it's hidden in its own way. You couldn't ask for a quieter spot."

"Okay. Let's go see it."

In the hallway as they left the library Jessica thought, *We're doing this together. That might be the craziest thing so far.* Exiting through the back door they found that the day had grown late. The shadows of the hills to the west had already crept beyond the house and only the tallest trees still touched the sunlight. The winds gusting through the branches and around the house made a constant rattling hiss.

Katie looked up from her work in a broccoli patch as they approached. She was wearing old work pants and a maroon sweatshirt and she'd braided her salt-and-pepper hair behind her head. Mr. McNulty called over the wind: "Katie, we're heading up the hill, to take a look at the rock."

"Oh? Sounds wonderful," she called. "Mind if I join you? I could do with a walk."

Mr. McNulty met Jessica's eyes. She shook her head slightly; she didn't want any more complications. "Well, the thing is," he called, "it—ahh—might not be safe...."

"What? Not safe?" Katie said, rising from her knees. "What do you mean, George? What's going on?"

He looked at Jessica again; she winced and shrugged, not knowing what to say. "Ahh—all right, then," he said. "Come along if you like. I'll tell you some things on the way."

"Well, this should be interesting." Katie dropped her gardener's gloves and walked with them under the citrus trees and onto a path that led to the back of the yard. The path ended at a gated fence made of tall wooden slats, warped and gray from sunlight and rain. Mr. McNulty unlatched the gate and held it as they crossed through.

Outside the fence only a dozen yards separated them from the base of the hills. The first slope rose quickly, dried grasses flowing in complicated wind patterns across the folds and hollows. A narrow trail, almost lost in the brush, snaked up the slope and across to the left until it vanished around a shoulder of the hill.

Mr. McNulty led them up the trail with Katie close behind; they were talking but Jessica couldn't make out the words. As they climbed the gusts grew wilder, whipping the grasses and bending long plant stems across the path. Jessica pushed the plants aside and tried to ignore her hair, which kept flying in several directions at once. When she finally managed to brush it back her scalp almost crackled with electricity.

The path leveled out near the shoulder of the hill, and as they turned the corner the gusts dropped away as abruptly as if someone had closed a door. They had entered a ravine, steep and narrow and sheltered from the wind. Jessica heard Katie say, "—wait so long to tell me? And don't you even *think* about asking me to go home. I am *not* going to sit there and twiddle my thumbs and hope nothing terrible happens out here."

"Fine enough—but this isn't my show," Mr. McNulty said.

"Oh. Yes, you're quite right." Katie turned to Jessica. "Jessica, dear, I seem to have poked my nose in uninvited—and I hardly know what to think, after hearing about it from George—but may I stay with you while you do this? Please be honest. I make a lot of noise with George but I'm actually happy to go back if it's for the best."

"No, please—stay if you want to," Jessica said. "I'd like that.

I just don't know if it'll be dangerous."

"Well, then I'd rather be here than elsewhere, thank you. And once we're done I hope you'll explain it all to me."

Just ahead the trail ended. Wedged into the back of the ravine was a rocky outcropping, a sandstone block studded with pebbles like walnuts in cookie dough. The trail had brought them to the top of the rock, a broad level space ten feet to a side, the surface scored by potholes and rain gullies. Mr. McNulty said, "This is the place. Lots of history around here. Some Chumash Indians told me there's an old gathering place not far away. They're aiming to acquire the land—or get it back, really. Asked if I'd help keep an eye on it in the meantime."

"Cool," Mitch said. He watched Jessica as she took a few steps onto the stone. "What do you think?"

Jessica tested the surface through her shoes. She sensed the strength of the stone, hard roots sunk deep into the hill, and her nose filled with earthy scents of grasses and sage. Looking up the slope she saw a single oak tree rooted at the crest, its trunk and the undersides of its branches washed with amber in the late sunlight. The air around her felt absolutely still, but above her the tree branches rocked and swayed and the leaves hissed in the unseen wind. The tree seemed unworldly, moving to rhythms from some other place or time. Jessica found it perfectly beautiful.

"It's just right," she said.

"Great," Mitch said. "What do we do?"

"Well...we could all sit down."

Mitch and Jessica sat quickly, Katie took a bit longer, and Mr. McNulty took longer still, muttering "Be thankful for young joints." Jessica's hands felt cold and she rubbed them on her pant legs. "Okay, umm...you know I'm gonna try to reach Mr. Peabody. I have to concentrate and it might take a while. I don't think you'll hear anything—but you might, I guess. That's about all I can tell you."

"Do what you have to do. We'll be here," Mr. McNulty said.

"If you need help, just holler," Mitch said.

"I will," Jessica said. "Well...here goes."

She rested her elbows on her knees and lowered her head into her hands. For a time she simply waited, eyes closed, not thinking of anything in particular, hearing the wind in the oak tree and letting her mind clear.

She thought back to the call from Ariel. She brought it up and let it ring in her head again, hearing the highest tones as they rose and fell, feeling the echoes and the deeper tones that rumbled underneath. She listened to it again and then again. She had thought she understood it earlier in the day but now there seemed a hint of something she couldn't see, a clarity that lay just out of reach. It teased at her but she couldn't quite grasp it.

She relaxed, ignoring the frustration, and listened once more. All at once it was there in front of her: the call had a shape. The sounds flowed and harmonized in a long complex curve like the arc of a bird's wing. She could see how it began, how it lifted and swelled, and how it narrowed to an end. And she knew instinctively how to fill it with a word.

It was time. Jessica spoke the name in her mind, slipping it into the shape and letting it go: "...*mmmmmmMMMMMIII-ISSSSSSSSTTTTEEERRRRRRRPPPPPEEEEAABBBBOOOOOD-DDDDYYYYYYYYyyyyyyyyy....*"

When the call trailed off she felt weary, suddenly. She knew the words had gone out but she had no idea where they had gone. She gathered strength to try it again.

Then three things happened, one after the other.

The rock beneath her shuddered like a sidewalk when a truck drives by. She heard Katie gasping and Mr. McNulty grunting, almost at the same moment. Then Mitch spoke in a sharp whisper: "Jessie...I think he heard you."

Chapter 8

Questions on the Hillside

JESSICA LOOKED UP, blinking, and saw Mr. Peabody.

He stood on the rock surface, just a few feet behind the gap between Jessica and Mr. McNulty. His appearance hadn't changed from the last time she'd seen him: hawkish face, thick hair swept back, a dark garment covering him from neck to ground. Jessica turned to the others, wondering if they could see what she was seeing; she found them all staring wide-eyed at their guest, Mitch with his mouth partly open.

The visitor inclined his head—like a nod, almost. When he spoke, his voice seemed to resonate in the rock and in her bones: "Jessica Blackwater."

She swallowed, finding that her tongue was dry. "Y-yes."

"You have hailed me," he said.

It took her a moment to understand. "Yes, sir...I g-guess I did."

"It was—not expected."

"Uh...yeah, sorry," she said. "It, uh, kind of surprised me too."

The visitor was silent, then said, "We must speak."

Jessica nodded. "I was—I hoped we could."

135

"Shall I—be welcomed, then?" he said. "Do you receive me, to this circle?"

Jessica stared at him, then looked to the others, hoping for some help. They still seemed in shock: Katie and Mitch couldn't pull their eyes away from Mr. Peabody and Mr. McNulty blinked at her with a glazed expression. She said, "Well...well yes, you're very welcome here—sir. Please join us."

He knelt in an impossibly smooth motion, flowing forward and down until his head was nearly level with Jessica's. Just as at the mansion the air around him shivered as he moved, making Jessica feel that an effort lay behind the image she was seeing, perhaps a greater effort than any of them imagined.

With his face just a few feet away Jessica couldn't help staring at the dark centers of his eyes. "We must speak," he said again.

"Uh—right," she said.

"Ariel is—in difficulty. You know this? She has called to you?"

"Yes. I heard her voice...this morning. It sounded like—like something was really wrong."

He seemed to watch her carefully. "I see that I was quick—too hasty—when we met. The themes were not clear to me. They are hidden even now."

Jessica wasn't sure what that meant, but it sort of sounded like an apology. "That's all right," she said. "I'm sorry I made a mess out of things...and it was my fault, you know. I hope Ariel didn't get in trouble."

He nodded once. "I will hear from you. There are passages to unfold before the movement will resolve. But first, perhaps, you wish to—acquaint me, with your companions."

Jessica blinked, then said, "Oh...of course. This is Mitch Carlucci, my best friend. And over there is Katie and Mr. McNulty. He's a teacher at our school, or he used to be. They're married."

The visitor inclined to them; they seemed to have recovered somewhat, and the introductions may have helped. Mr. McNulty said, "We're, ahh...honored. Certainly. But I have to tell you, we don't quite know the, ahh—etiquette, for this sort of thing."

"Yes."

"If it's all right: we've been told your name is 'Mr. Peabody.' Is that the case?"

The visitor said, "It is a given name—chosen, by Ariel. My true name she could not receive."

"Oh," Katie said. "She couldn't understand it? Or pronounce it?"

"Yes. In 'Mr. Peabody' she found—simplicity, I believe. Comfort. I have accepted it, for her sake."

Mitch spoke up. "Sir, I hope this isn't rude...but we can see that you're not, you know, human."

His expression did not change. "I am not."

"Okay. Can we ask who you are, exactly? Like, you're not an angel, are you?"

He was silent for a time. "The word is—not simple. Once among you, it may have spoken of my kind, in part. The intent was larger, more certain. Now among you, the intent is lost, I do not hear it."

"Oh," Mitch said. "Does that mean 'no'?"

The visitor considered again. "I have heard a deep-rooted word, in your tongue. It is *seraph*. Do you know it?"

"Ah," Katie said, almost as a sigh. "*Seraph*, singular; from the Latin *seraphim*, plural. From the Hebrew, originally. Does it suit you?"

He inclined his head. "It will serve."

Jessica figured it was her turn. "Sir, what about Ariel, then? Is she...like you? One of your kind?"

"No," he said.

"So she's human? From our world?"

"Yes."

Jessica looked at the others. "Well, for a long time now we've been trying to figure out where she came from and how she can do what she does. And I have to find out what's happened to her. Could you—can I ask you to tell us all of that?"

He was quiet for a long space. "I will tell what I can," he said. "Much of it may be—troublesome, to transpose. Not easily spoken. But I will tell it, so that you hear what is known and what has not yet been seen."

It seemed to Jessica that his eyes glistened as he began. "Let us say," he said, "that some among my kind are—gifted, in a certain manner. We may call these gifted ones *Harkeners*. Let us say that their gift is—an awareness. A perceiving. Their work is to discern passages, or turns, or phrases, within and among the living worlds. The Harkeners hear these things and search for the themes that link them—bind them—to the great story, the One Story, that unfolds in every place, and whose end is not yet seen.

"Now at a certain time, some among the Harkeners became troubled. They had glimpsed a movement, a coming-and-going, that was unknown to them. It followed no rhythm—no pattern—that had been heard among us. No theme could be perceived. It was a new thing, and we are not accustomed to new things.

"You will understand, that many shared a—desire, to learn more. To me was given the task of seeking. I began to search and to follow, and to wait. The seeking was not simple—my quarry had some sense of me, and moved when I approached. But in this I found a gift: I came to see a pattern in the fleeing. I moved ahead to a certain place, to greet it when it arrived."

Jessica said, "And it was Ariel?"

The seraph tilted his head, as if to say: *not quite.* "It was a young woman," he said. "This was not expected. From time to

138

time, I have heard, a few among your kind have slipped between worlds. But the slipping had been a mishap, or an—intervention. Here was one who moved freely, by her own will. And yet this was not the most curious thing."

He seemed to hesitate. "It is best now if you see what I have seen. Will you permit me?"

"Umm...sure," Jessica said. "Whatever you want."

A breeze ruffled past her face. In the center of the circle the air began to swirl, spiraling in and upward like a slow whirlwind. The spinning picked up speed and the air seemed to flicker. Pale streams of light slid upward from the stone, twisting in the turning air; they folded into each other, lacing and braiding in odd patterns, until all at once they settled into a recognizable shape.

"Oh my," Katie said.

"Cool," Mitch said.

Suspended in the whirlwind was the image of young girl, small and transparent like a reflection in a window. Her feet were bare, her hair short and dark, and she wore cut-off jeans and a large shirt. She crouched in an awkward position, blinking and flinching as the image turned.

"Is that Ariel?" Mitch said.

"Well—sort of," Jessica said. The girl seemed different from the Ariel she knew. Her skin looked dirty and her hair was partly stringy and partly matted. Her eyes held a wild look, almost a kind of desperation, and she moved as though trying to hide, squeezing into a narrow space where she wouldn't be seen. "Sir, is this how you found her?" she said.

"Yes. She was not well," the seraph said. "There was damage in her body, and in her—breath. Her spirit. She did not fear me, I believe, but she was fearful of—discovery, of being found. As though she fled from something I had not seen.

"Her speech at first was broken, weak—but in time we heard each other. I sought to learn her story. Here I met disappointment: her remembrance also was broken. She could not explain where she began, or how she had come to travel. She could not remember her name."

"Seriously?" Jessica said.

"Yes. The damage was—profound."

"But sir," Mitch said, "she had her pipes, her instrument, when you found her?"

"Yes."

"Do you know how she got them?"

"No. It is possible she made them herself."

"But that's...." Jessica trailed off as she looked at the image, the cowering creature who seemed so distant from the Ariel she knew. Every answer had three or four questions waiting behind it. It was becoming frustrating.

The seraph said, "I took counsel with my kind. We did not know what could be done—yet we would not abandon her. To me was given another charge: if my presence was accepted, I would be a guide for her, a guardian. I had no knowledge of such a task, nor had any of us. But it must be done."

The image unraveled into sparks and strands of light. The motes spiraled in the wind and drew together into another shape: Ariel again, looking much more as Jessica remembered her. She sat playing her pipes (though the image gave no sound), looking calm and peaceful, her eyes clear and bright.

"Ariel received this," the seraph said. "She remained with me under my protection. In time I saw healing, in her manner and her spirit. Her words returned to her and she spoke freely. She chose a name for me, as you have heard. She chose 'Ariel' for herself."

"Really? She just picked it?" Jessica said.

"Yes."

"Weird," Mitch said. "It's a funny choice."

"Perhaps. Much has been uncertain, perhaps because our kinds are—distinct. This did not trouble her, I believe. She sought to learn from me. She listened to passages that are sung among us—movements of charity, and of—grace, and began to play them. She came to be called 'Songweaver' by those who heard. She asked to join my tasks, to assist me. In this her acts were often unexpected...at times, nearly unwise. But she chose well. Her intent was simple, undivided.

"Then came a measure that I do not understand."

The image in the air came apart again and reshaped. Now Ariel lay on her back with one leg crossed over a knee, her foot bouncing as she played a tune. Nearby in the image stood a dry thicket; a few of the plants moved aside and a girl pushed through, looking surprised. Ariel turned towards her and the girl seemed to speak.

"Hey, Jessie, that's you!" Mitch said.

"Oh...yeah," Jessica said. "I get it. It's the day I met Ariel. Sir, how did you know about it?"

"Ariel told it, after your last journey with her," he said.

"Oh, right. But you said you didn't understand."

"Yes."

"It's no big deal. I decided to walk to school that day and I heard her playing the music. It was an accident."

"You saw Ariel and you heard her," the seraph said, "though she was not within your world. That is a rare gift. You have a capacity for—the traveling."

"Well, not like Ariel," she said.

"You sent a hail that is heard only among my kind."

"Yeah—I guess so."

"You are gifted in this manner," the seraph said, "and at a certain time, at a certain place, as Ariel was playing her music, you chose to pass nearby."

Mitch made a *huh* sound. "Yeah, when you put it like that... awfully big coincidence."

Katie said, "So if not an accident, what then? What else was going on?"

"I cannot speak it," the seraph said. "But greater purposes may be at work, passing deeper than I may see. I will honor them if they can be heard. Perhaps in time more will become known, to you and to all."

Jessica felt uncomfortable with the discussion. She never liked hearing people talk about her and she'd gotten tired of watching her face in the image. "All right, that's for later," she said. "Right now we still need to know what's happened to Ariel. She's in trouble, right?"

The seraph said, "She has—journeyed, of her own will, to a certain place. She does not belong there...and has desired to leave, but she cannot. She called to you while she was able—while she had not forgotten."

Mitch said, "So where is it? Can you show us?"

The image came apart again, unwinding and fragmenting, and when the pieces settled the air held only a misty blur, a gray fog. Jessica squinted to peer through but could only make out dark bands or patches drifting below the clouds.

"I cannot show more than this," the seraph said. "It is a place I cannot see."

"But what is it?" Mitch said.

"The true name is not known to you," he said. "It is a place of loss, and of—forgetting. It is Desolation, or Hope's End. Or simply Oblivion."

"Sounds bad," Mitch said. "Like a place for dead people."

"Yes."

There was another silence. Jessica said, "What—what do you mean, sir?"

"For your kind, it is a place of the lost, who are not in the flesh," he said. "It is a place of the dead."

Jessica stared at him while a sinking feeling took hold in her stomach. She heard Katie whisper *Oh my*, but didn't look at her. She tried to think of the next question she wanted to ask. The seraph spoke before she was ready.

"Now I must ask you," he said, "why she has done this."

Jessica blinked at him. "You're asking *me*?"

"Yes."

"Sir...I don't have any idea. She didn't tell me. I haven't seen her since that time at the mansion."

"And yet. In Ariel's act there is—a hidden phrase. A passage I have not heard. I believe it lies between you."

"I don't...I don't know what you mean. She must have told you everything we did. She came to see me when she could. We went on the jobs together and we talked sometimes. That's all."

The seraph watched her. "There was...a binding, perhaps. A promise."

"Well, I don't—well, okay," Jessica said. "One thing like that. The time we helped the king at the castle—we were talking on the hillside afterward. Ariel promised she would always try to help me, no matter what. I said the same thing. That's all. And she said—then she said—"

Jessica broke off and brought a hand to her mouth. "Oh no," she said in a small voice. "Oh no, oh no...."

"What?" Mitch said.

She turned to him as though moving underwater. "It's Brad," she said. "I think she was looking for Brad."

Mitch's eyes widened. "No way."

Her throat tightened as she pushed the words out. "I talked about how long he's been gone—I was afraid he might even be dead. She said she would try to find him. She said she'd do anything, go places that—that are hard to reach. Something like that. Places where other people can't go...." Jessica stopped there and stared into the blurred image that turned in the middle of the circle.

"I hear it now," the seraph said. "The theme that was hidden. A covenant between you, a bond of compassion. It led Ariel to this act when she did not know the danger. I regret...I did not hear it sooner."

They all fell quiet then. Jessica watched the gray fog and felt the cold from the rock seeping into her legs.

Mr. McNulty cleared his throat. "Sir, you said you can't go to this place?"

"Yes. My kind cannot be present. I cannot enter there, as you could not enter a—shadow, or a stone."

"Ah. That's...unfortunate."

"But is she really lost then?" Katie said. "Can't anything be done?"

"I have sought counsel, among my kind," the seraph said. "We seek another resolve, a better resolution. Yet she remains beyond our reach."

Jessica still watched the mist that turned in the whirlwind. Now and then she thought she caught glimpses of distant shapes, as though looking down from a great height. She tried to imagine getting trapped or lost in a place like that, to feel that you were never going to leave. She decided she didn't want to think about it anymore.

"Sir, you can't go to that place," she said, "but one of us could, right?"

The seraph spoke with measured words. "To enter there—to be present—is possible for your kind. But none of you could travel there, as Ariel does."

"No. But you could send me, right?"

She heard Mitch mutter *"Jessie"* in a tight voice; she ignored it. The seraph bent his head and said, "It is...not impossible. But I could not ask it."

"That's all right," Jessica said. "I'm the one asking. Would you send me there, right away, so I can help Ariel get out?"

"Now, hold a minute," Mr. McNulty said.

"Yeah," Mitch said, "hold on *two* minutes. Are you *nuts*?"

"No. I really have to do it."

Mitch waved at the gray fog. "What—you have to disappear? You have to go away forever?"

"I have to *help* her," Jessica said. "You see what it looks like. How do you think she feels right now? And she's there because of *me*. Well, I made a promise too, like she did, and I'm going to keep it."

"But listen now," Mr. McNulty said, "you know you can't do the kinds of things Ariel does."

"Yeah," Mitch said, "so if she can't get out, you'll *both* get lost. How are you supposed to change anything?"

"I...I don't know yet. When I'm with her we'll figure it out. We always did when we were on the jobs."

They didn't look convinced. Before they could speak again she turned to Mr. Peabody. "Sir, does it make sense, what I'm saying? If I go to Ariel is there a chance I could bring her back?"

He watched her again with his dark gaze; she did her best to meet it. When he spoke, he seemed to be musing aloud. "Fidelity," he said, "and sacrifice. So young, yet you hear the themes. There is hope in that. But can you know where they will take you? When strength is lost, will you hear, even then? And know what must be done?"

She had to be honest, then. "Sir...I don't really understand what you mean when you say those things. But my friend's in trouble and I have to help her. That's all."

As the seraph regarded her his image began to waver, like the tree on the crest of the hill when it shivered in the wind. For the first time, Jessica had a sense that Mr. Peabody might not be entirely *there*—that a part of him, or even most of him, might be in a place she couldn't see. She wondered if the shivering meant that something was happening in that other place. Like a discussion, maybe. Or a decision.

The seraph's figure steadied. "I may send you," he said. "It will not be simple. There will be a—journey. You may begin now if you choose it."

"Now wait, just wait," Mitch said, giving Jessica a hard look. "Okay, sir—if she's going, we have to go with her."

"What?" Jessica said.

"Mr. McNulty and I already decided, sir. If Jessica takes a risk, we have to do it too. The whole mess is partly our fault, so it's only fair."

"Ahh...right," Mr. McNulty said.

"So, is that okay? You can send us along too?"

The seraph was still for a time. "In part," he said. "You may join her for some—portion, of the journey. I cannot say more."

"Umm...all right. If that's it. And thanks."

"Will you go at once?" the seraph said.

"If you don't mind," Mr. McNulty said, "Katie and I ought to —ahh—take care of a couple things at home." (Jessica heard Mitch mutter under his breath, *And I gotta use the bathroom.*) "Would that be a problem?"

"It would not."

"Fine. Our place is at the base of the hill. Could you meet us outside the fence?"

"I will," the seraph said. Before he completed the words his figure seemed to pull inward or withdraw, slipping away and vanishing in little more than a second. The floating mist blew to shreds as the whirlwind lifted up and drifted off the stone.

All at once it was very dark—the sun must have set while they were talking, though Jessica hadn't noticed. She couldn't see the others' faces and could barely make out their outlines.

"Whoa," Mitch said. It seemed like a decent summary.

"Guys," Jessica said, "you've been so great, but you don't have to do this with me. Really."

"I rather think we do, after all that," Katie said. "We won't abandon you now."

"Yep," Mr. McNulty said. When he fell quiet, Jessica pictured him pushing up his glasses. "Though I have to say, however you look at it, we're in way over our heads."

"Yeah, afraid so," Jessica said.

146

After another moment, Mitch said, "I'll bet nobody brought a flashlight."

They didn't need one, as it turned out: the moon had cleared the eastern horizon, giving them enough light to find the trail and follow it away from the rock. The winds hit them as they left the ravine, but the long slope looked almost bright under the open sky as they walked the downhill path to the McNultys' yard.

Inside the house Mitch headed for a bathroom and Jessica asked if she could use the phone. "Help yourself," Katie said, "there's one in the library if you want privacy."

In the back room she found the telephone, half-buried under magazines on a bookshelf. It looked like an antique, heavy and black with an actual dial you had to spin with your finger. Jessica had never worked a phone like that so she practiced a few times before she picked up the handset and dialed her home number. The recorder picked up after two rings and played her mother's voice: "Hello, you've reached the Blackwaters. Sorry to miss you, but please leave your number...." Jessica started talking after the beep.

"Hi Mom, it's me. I'm at the McNultys'—I came over with Mitch after school. We've been hanging out—just gabbing and stuff...." And what else could she say, exactly? *We went up in the hills and talked with Mr. Peabody, who's sort of an angel.* "Anyway, everything's fine. Not sure when I'll be home...." *Because I'm traveling to Oblivion to find my invisible friend.* "But, I, uhh... wanted you to know. So you don't need to worry. I'll see you soon." *Unless I never come back.* "Hope you had a good day...love you. See you. Bye."

She muttered, "Well, that was lame," as she hung up the handset. She wished now she'd found a way to tell her mother what had been going on the last several weeks. "I always think of this stuff too late," she said as she left the room.

No one was waiting in the living room or the kitchen so she

walked out through the back door. Mitch stood outside on the garden path with his jacket zipped against the wind and his hands stuffed in his pockets. She nodded to him and they both watched for the McNultys.

After a while Mitch said, "Uh, Jessie?"

"Yeah?"

"I don't want to lose you, okay?"

Jessica smiled, almost embarrassed. "Okay. And I don't want to, you know...get lost, either."

"Good."

The wind gusted noisily, then calmed itself. Mitch said, "This isn't just about Ariel, right?"

Jessica sighed. "Right."

"You want to know if Brad's really there."

"Well...I'm not sure I *want* to know. But I *gotta* know." She hunched her shoulders and shivered in the chill. "I think Ariel saw that better than me."

A minute later the back door opened and Katie stepped out; she had changed into a long heavy skirt and a denim jacket. Mr. McNulty followed after her. "Katie decided to pack some food," he said.

"Dried fruit and beef jerky," Katie said, patting a pocket. "And don't you complain about it, George. We don't know where we're going or how long we'll be gone. Better to be prepared."

"Whatever," Mr. McNulty said. "Let's do this."

They walked down the path and out through the gate, Mr. McNulty latching it behind them. The winds blew so strong now that Jessica stood with her feet apart so that they wouldn't push her off balance. Overhead the night sky shone almost painfully clear, the stars sparkling like bits of shattered glass.

Mitch said, "Do you need to do anyth—"

Under their feet the ground trembled and Jessica felt her

insides lift as though she were on a rollercoaster. She shivered and saw Mr. Peabody standing a few feet away.

"All is ready," he said. "Are you prepared?"

Jessica nodded. "I think so, sir. Ready as we're gonna be."

The seraph inclined his head. "I send you to one who will open the way. Go in mercy, Jessica Blackwater. In mercy and in hope." He appeared to spread out his arms, then, or open up some other sort of limbs, and from the darkness of his cloak there erupted a blaze of light. Jessica squinted against it and felt herself start to spin.

Chapter 9

The Waters Beneath the Worlds

AS THE BRIGHTNESS faded and Jessica felt solid ground under her feet again, she blinked several times and looked around her.

She stood with the others in a kind of clearing, a grassy patch in a circle of dark fir trees. The grass blades were tangled and damp with dew and most of the tree branches drooped so low that she couldn't see beyond them. Off to one side a single opening broke the circle, an arching branch with stepping stones beneath it like an entrance to a tunnel; otherwise, there was nothing to see and certainly no one to meet them. "Huh," she said. "This isn't what—"

She broke off when she saw Katie shivering and blinking and Mr. McNulty bending over with his hands on his knees, breathing deeply. "Oh no," she said, "are you—are you guys okay?"

Mr. McNulty straightened, speaking between breaths. "Just, ahh—give me another minute." Katie's eyes seemed to focus then and she nodded. "We're—we're all right, I think," she said. "What about you?"

"Oh, fine. It's, uh...it gets easier, once you've done it a few times."

Mitch, by contrast, seemed completely unaffected, looking wide-eyed around the clearing and almost bouncing on his toes. "Oh wow, oh wow," he said. "This is so *great*. It's the coolest thing ever!"

"Yeah, well...let's wait and see, before you say that," Jessica said.

In the silence after she spoke, she could hear a slow patter of dewdrops falling from the branches. Mr. McNulty said, "Do you know where we are, by any chance?"

"Umm—no. Not really."

"We're supposed to meet someone?" Mitch said. "Or do you have to do something first?"

"I'm not sure. Mr. Peabody didn't tell us much." She nodded towards the arching branch. "I guess we could walk through there and have a look, as long as we don't get lost."

They followed the path into the shadow of the trees, where the trail began to drift downhill. The stones turned into steps, shallow steps in a broad stairway, dropping down between mounded banks that were lined with trees and carpeted with gray-green moss. Branches overhead crowded out the light and Jessica couldn't tell where the steps were taking them, but there didn't seem any reason to turn back.

"We found ourselves in a dark wood," Katie murmured as they walked.

Mr. McNulty *hmffed* and said "Interesting thought," but Jessica wasn't sure what she meant. "Umm...is that a quote or something?"

"Sort of," Katie said. "There's a line from a poem: 'In the middle of my life's journey, I woke to find myself in a dark wood, for the straight way had been lost.'"

"Dante's *Inferno*," Mr. McNulty said. "The opening lines."

"Oh—I see. That's, umm...not very cheerful," Jessica said.

"No, not at all," Katie said. "Jessica, I have to tell you, there's a part of me that would very much like to talk you out of this, but I know it's wrong to try and I won't even bother. But I wish, at least, I knew more than I do. I wish I knew what you were getting yourself into."

"Well, that makes two of us," Jessica said. She tried to make the words sound breezy and confident but they came out awkward instead, and she clenched her jaw to keep from saying anything else.

The trees grew more sparsely as they neared the bottom of the stairs. Through the branches Jessica could see water in the distance, a lake or a placid river. When the steps flattened out, they walked out from the trees onto a shelf of rock that ran down several yards to the water's edge. The lake stretched ahead of them and on either side, hardly a ripple on the smooth surface, a thin fog drifting in wisps not far offshore.

Riding at the shoreline was a wooden boat, a vessel with carved rails and a raised prow and an equally tall stern, resting like a curled leaf on the water. A gray-haired man stood beside the boat lighting a lantern that hung from the arching prow. He wore a long wool coat, wine-colored in the pale light, and a wooden pole was propped against his shoulder. He closed the lamp and nodded to them.

"Good day to you," he said.

"And to you," said Mr. McNulty. He looked uncomfortable as he eyed the boat. "If you don't—ahh—mind my asking...do we need to pay a toll, by any chance?"

The man seemed amused. "I see: you wonder if I'm the boatman on the river Acheron, the ferryman for the dead. Well, I'm not he, I'm happy to say. And this is not that place, not nearly so dismal." He offered a hand. "Call me Hunter. I'm here because I know the way."

He clasped hands with each of them in turn. Jessica thought his face had a weathered look, with deep creases around his eyes and wrinkles that ran down beneath his cropped gray beard. Mitch asked, "Should we introduce ourselves?" and Hunter shook his head: "Not to worry—I've heard who you are and why you've come." When he took Jessica's hand he said, "And you'll be Jessica, the young woman who seeks Oblivion."

Holding the rod with one hand like a staff he dropped to one knee in front of her. His face was close enough now that Jessica could count the lines at the corners of his dark eyes, and she also saw something odd: the deep creases in his cheek that she had taken for wrinkles were actually scars. They ran in ragged lines down into his beard like claw marks from some animal. The hand that held the rod looked equally scarred, and she winced, thinking about the wounds. He cocked his head to one side, watching her.

"It's a brave thing you mean to do," he said.

"Oh—thank you," she said.

"But likely as not it's all for nothing. Your friend has lost herself in a place she doesn't understand, and now you want to follow, though you know even less than she. Perhaps it's less brave than simply foolish."

Jessica squeezed her fists, bristling inside. "I'm—you may be right, sir," she said. "But I don't think it matters. My friend's in trouble and I have to help her. And really, I'm the whole reason she's in this mess. So I have to do this. I don't think I have a choice."

Hunter arched an eyebrow. "No choice? That's hardly ever the case, I'd say. But however that may be, there are things I must tell you. Will you hear them now?"

"Yes. Please."

He gestured a hand out towards the lake. "Not far from here is a gateway into Oblivion. It lies in a stretch of water beyond the barrier walls and the forest-lake. It's a gate that may be passed by those in the flesh. It's not been used in many a long year, but it will open. If your heart is settled to go there, I'll take you. Nothing will hinder you.

"But there's a danger beyond the getting there and getting back. Oblivion, you see, is a place of forgetting. Do you know what that means?"

"Well—Mr. Peabody mentioned it, but I wasn't sure what he meant."

"It's just this: Oblivion is the death of memory. Those who go there forget their lives, every part of their lives. Memories fade, the past slips away, thoughts vanish, until nothing is left, or very nearly nothing."

"Oh—I didn't know," she said. "It sounds terrible."

"Yeah," Mitch chimed in. "Like disappearing, only inside-out."

"But sir, what about Ariel, then? She went there, but she wasn't, umm...like the others...."

She knew what the answer would be when she met his eyes. "It would make no difference," he said. "The forgetting comes upon all, without exception. Whether or not they happen to be alive."

"Oh...oh no."

"Yes. It's likely she would not have known the danger. By the time she understood, it would have already been too late."

Jessica remembered the sound of Ariel's voice when she'd heard her calling, the feeling of desperation in her tone—like a last cry, like the last thing she knew how to do. It made sense now but Jessica didn't want to think about it too deeply. Hunter continued, "Be sure of this: what has happened to your friend will happen to you, if you go. How quickly it might come I can't say. But if you falter or if you linger too long, you will forget everything that matters, including the way out. You will be lost beyond reach, and beyond hope.

"And last of all know this: you may gamble your own life but not another's. If you go, you go alone."

Mitch reacted before Jessica could speak: "Wait—you can't mean that—we're in this together." And Katie said, "We want to help, it's why we came this far."

Hunter shook his head. "You're more than kind to ask, but it won't do. You could not delay the forgetting or make her task easier; you could only hinder or distract, and if she fails you would all be lost. I'm sorry. She must risk no life but her own."

He tilted his head again. "Now perhaps you have a choice, after all. You can return home without shame after what you've heard. But if you go forward, you must choose freely, with your eyes open and your heart clear. So what will you do?"

Jessica caught sight of Mitch from the corner of an eye: he shook his head, his lips pressed into a narrow line, as though to say: *Don't. Don't do it. Don't go.* A small thing, really, but the moment unloosed the doubts she'd been holding back, walled off in some corner of her mind. They rushed through her now like a panicked crowd: Mitch was right and she'd been silly not to see it; she had no idea what she was doing; it was all point-less, ridiculous, doomed from the start; she was just wasting everyone's time. She bit her lip and squeezed her hands tighter, trying to stiffen herself inside. "I'm—I'm not sure what to tell you, sir," she managed to say. "I can't abandon my friend. I can't do that."

"Of course."

"But it sounds like you're saying this is impossible."

He shook his head. "Whether it is or not, is more than I can say."

"Is it me, then?" she said, hating the words. "I mean, am I just not strong enough, or old enough? Or smart enough?"

"Such things don't matter, not here." Hunter folded his hands together and the creases around his eyes seemed to deepen. "Listen, now: here's the heart of it. You want to do a great mercy, and that's well and good—but such things are never simple. There is always a cost. Whether you return or not there will be loss—great loss, perhaps—and you will not be what you were. If that is too much to bear then the task is not for you. Can you see that?"

"Yes...I think so," Jessica said, adding to herself: *But I don't think it tells me what I want to know.* She struggled to find the words for a last question; she glanced at the scars on Hunter's face and had a sudden thought.

"Then sir," she said, "if I could ask one more thing—if you were in my place right now, would you go to Oblivion?"

Hunter said, "Ahh," with a raised eyebrow. He looked away, long enough for Jessica to worry that she'd pushed too far; but when he spoke again, she felt a warmth in his eye and a note of sorrow in his voice.

"If I were in your place, with a friend in such danger—yes. I would go," he said. "I would go where the road took me and pay the price. Take that for what it is; but it may be that love would ask no less."

"Oh," Jessica said. *Is that my answer, then?* she wondered. *Well, it has to be, it's all I've got.* "Then, sir, if it's all right—" her voice stuck, but she kept going, "—if it's all right, I'd like to go find my friend now."

She thought Hunter might argue but she was disappointed. He only watched her under his brows, then nodded and said "Very good" with a kind of satisfaction.

He rose to his feet and spoke to the others. "We can take no more time here. You know that Jessica will enter Oblivion alone, but any of you may come as far as the last gate. The boat will carry all of you if you wish it."

Katie looked shaken but she didn't hesitate: "I'm sure we'd all want that," she said. Hunter steadied the boat with a hand while the four of them stepped aboard, Katie and Mr. McNulty finding seats near the bow while Mitch and Jessica sat on carved benches in the middle. Hunter stepped in last, the boat rocking as he moved to the stern. He planted the pole against the lake bottom; the boat scraped forward and rocked sharply to the left, and all at once they floated freely. He planted the pole again and the boat slipped across the water.

This is it, Jessica thought. *I'm really doing this. And it was my choice.*

She had never ridden in a small boat before and the movement felt strange at first, so smooth it seemed nearly unnatural —if she ignored the splashing of the pole, she could have believed they were standing still. Within a dozen yards the lake fog closed around them, and when she glanced back the shoreline had already been lost. The glow of the lamp floated ahead of them but it brightened no more than a few feet of water.

Mitch sat across from her staring into the mist. She reached over and bumped his knee. "Hey," she said quietly, "you mad at me?"

"Nah," he said.

"You sure?"

"Yeah—I know you gotta do this. I don't like it, but I get it." Then after a moment, "But if you don't come back, you're *really* in trouble. Okay?"

"Okay, that's fair."

Mitch spoke to Hunter then. "Sir...could I ask something? Because none of us really knows where we are right now. I mean, where this place is. Or *what* it is. Is that something you can tell us?"

"Ah. Not a simple question," the man said.

"Yeah, I was afraid of that. But it's not our world and it's not Oblivion, right?"

"Yes, that much can be said." He switched the pole from one side to the other. "This isn't quite a world in its own right. Perhaps you've heard about shared places, lands between the worlds—or *beneath* them, some might say. Middle places, common grounds, where the great worlds have footholds."

"Umm...no, I haven't, exactly. But is that what this is? You make it sound like a crossroads, almost."

"You might say so. A place where many paths cross. A traveler who knows the paths may go nearly anywhere from here. And likewise, those who are careless may easily lose their way."

"Yeah, I believe it. I wasn't planning to take chances." As he spoke the boat rode into a thicker patch of fog and the temperature seemed to drop several degrees. Jessica fumbled with her jacket but the mist thinned again before she could connect the zipper. Two more pushes from the pole and they rode out into a stretch of clear water.

At the bow Katie said "Oh my," and Mr. McNulty grunted his agreement. Ahead of the boat Jessica saw a tangle of green, a wall of foliage that rose directly from the lake. It looked for all the world like a vast irregular hedge, with roots as thick as branches and branches as gnarled as roots, rising forty feet or more and running off to the distance on either side. A few stray branches stretched out like canopies over the water, shading the pale light and muffling the sounds.

"I can't see an end to it," Katie said, looking to the sides, and Jessica said, "Me neither."

Mitch said to Hunter, "Sir, is this the barrier wall you mentioned?"

"Just so," he said.

"And on the other side...?"

"Not what you think. Something very different, as you'll see."

Off to the right Jessica spotted a small break, a dark entrance in the wall like the mouth of a cave. Hunter guided the boat towards the gap and poled them through the opening. They entered an arched tunnel that stretched further than the reach of the lantern light. Tangled roots and looping branches formed the walls and the air felt thick and musty like a damp cellar.

After a few boat lengths Jessica saw something ahead in the water: a dark column, a pillar made of ebony-colored wood. Odd designs had been engraved into the surface, knots and spiraled patterns that made no sense to her. Beyond the pillar the passage ended: thick branches formed a rough frame like the sides of a doorway, and inside the frame vines and roots had tangled into a solid mass. There didn't seem enough space for a mouse to pass, much less a person or a boat.

Hunter spoke as the boat slowed. "Mitch, I'd like your help here. On the pillar near the waterline there's an iron ring. Catch it if you would and hold us steady."

Mitch caught the ring and held on with both hands. "What is this, sir?" he said.

"The first gate. There'll be two more along the way." Bracing his feet in the boat he brought the pole up from the water and swung an end sharply against the pillar. The wood thrummed with a hollow tone like a note from a pipe organ; Jessica felt it shiver in the planks of the boat and tremble through the air. Hunter struck twice more, each blow landing on a different carved figure, the three tones harmonizing into a single chord.

As the tones died Jessica heard a rustling, whispering sound. Inside the frame of branches the vines were in motion, slipping and slithering around each other, untangling and pulling back, gradually opening a gap from bottom to top.

"*Very* cool," Mitch said.

"And the tones were the key," Mr. McNulty said.

"Just like we thought. Well, not *exactly* like we thought."

When the vines came to rest the boat had space enough to pass. Hunter slipped the pole into the water and drove them forward through the passage. Not far beyond the gate, Jessica could see a bright half-circle that looked like the end of the tunnel. A thick root arched above the opening with streamers of moss hanging like a ragged curtain. Hunter did not slow as they approached, poling them through the streamers and out into open water.

Jessica looked around, blinking. It was brighter there than she had expected, brighter than on the outside. She could tell that the lake extended in every direction, and in every direction there were trees, but she couldn't focus well enough to see them clearly.

She heard Mitch say "*Whoa*" in a low voice, as though the word had been pushed out of him. When her eyes finally focused, she whispered "*Whoa*" along with him.

If the hedge behind them had been enormous then the trees ahead were almost unimaginable. Jessica had once hiked through a redwood forest, with a grove of giant sequoia trees that had seemed impossibly tall; but the trees in front of her looked twice as large as any sequoia, and twice as large again. They towered over the boat with trunks wider than school buildings, wider than football fields, rising and rising with hardly a branch anywhere in sight. Jessica climbed them with her eyes, up and up, hundreds of feet, a thousand feet before the treetops lost themselves in a haze that drifted high like a morning fog. She stared until the vision made her dizzy and she grabbed the rail of the boat to keep from falling backwards.

Mr. McNulty muttered, "Unbelievable. That's all."

"Yes," Katie said. "But there they are."

Mitch spoke in a low voice. "Are they really trees? How could they be trees? Maybe they're something we've never heard of."

Jessica spoke to Hunter: "Can you tell us, sir? What *is* this place?"

Something had changed in the man's face, a brightness in his eyes she hadn't seen before. "A place like none other," he said as he poled them forward. "A place where worlds are born."

They rode along a lane of water flowing ahead without a

161

break, through ranks of trees like pillars for the sky. "No one, I think, could give you the whole truth of this place," Hunter said. "But here's the tale that is told: for every world that has life within it, that life begins here, in these waters. A small thing at first, no greater than a seed, falling here and taking root. It grows and thrives as a sapling will thrive, and when the time is ripe it reaches beyond this place, seeking its own country—a world barren until that time. When it finds and joins with it the world quickens, begins to live and breathe."

"So, you mean..." Mitch said, looking around him, "these trees—they all belong to different worlds?"

"Just so. Somewhere in the heights, it's said, they reach their own lands and seas, they nourish the soil and sweeten the winds. It's a picture, I warn you, and perhaps not the heart of it —but it may speak true enough."

They rode out from the narrow lane into a wider expanse of water, a pond or a clearing among the trees. Light from the high mists glimmered off ripples on the surface, and on every side trees receded into the distance, the furthest trunks shadowed like faerie towers in the haze.

"So many of them," Jessica murmured. "So many worlds."

"So many lives," Katie said. "So many stories."

"But they're all connected, right?" Mitch said. "They all begin in the same place. Right here."

"Can't even imagine it," Mr. McNulty said. "Too big to get your head around, if it's all true."

Hunter poled them to a lane of water that led away from the clearing. Jessica had a dozen questions in her head but she didn't feel like talking now. She thought about what Hunter had said and watched the trees as they passed, wondering at how different they were. Some looked massive and ancient, others so delicate they might have been made of paper. One tree had roots that had shaped themselves into tunnels and caves, dark openings that gave out echoes like waves on a shore.

Another appeared to be surrounded with glowing specks like fireflies, all drifting upward in unison, and though Jessica watched for a time she couldn't tell where they came from or where they were going.

The forest seemed to have its own scent, a spiced smell like sagebrush or rosemary. It was growing stronger and Jessica began to think it drifted from one direction, somewhere off to the left. They came to a wider passage, a long avenue with trees spaced evenly on either hand, and here a breeze blew from the left side. Mitch lifted his head, sniffing the air. "You smell that?" he said.

"Uh-huh," Jessica said. "Like a flower garden."

"Or a spice house. But I don't think anyone's cooking here."

"Yeah. So, what is it? Do you know, sir?" she said to Hunter, who had stopped poling and had turned his face to the breeze.

"Yes," he said, breathing in. "The heart of the lake. An island, like a great hill standing above the waters, with flowering plants that grow nowhere else. The waters of the lake begin there, rising from deep springs and flowing out to the trees."

"Oh, that's wonderful," Jessica said. "Are we going there?"

"No, we cannot. We'll only pass at a distance."

The scents strengthened as they rode further, sometimes reminding Jessica of rose or jasmine but often richer than anything she could name, and she felt lightheaded when she breathed too deep. The water had been changing along with the air: pale streaks now crossed the surface, narrow bands of light divided by the shadows of the trees. To the left in the distance Jessica could see a brighter glow like sunlight in a forest clearing. Something was out there, something that filled an open space in the lake, but the trees grew more closely in that direction and she couldn't see clearly beyond them.

Mitch slid to her side of the boat. "Is it there? Can you see it?" he said.

"I don't know."

"It's gotta be right there."

"Well, I can't tell," she said, just as a gap opened through the trees.

It opened briefly, barely the length of a held breath, but time enough to glimpse what lay beyond it. Jessica saw a slope that rose from the lake in terraces almost entirely clothed in green—spreading shrubs and arched trees and braids of hanging vines, dark like ivy or pale like beech trees, and every plant seemed in bloom, streaked with yellow and violet and brilliant orange. She saw streams running down the slopes, tumbling off terraces and drifting like mist when they reached waters of the lake. She saw paths that threaded up from the shore through the green like stairways cut into stone; her eyes traced one path as it wound to the top of the hill. There at the summit stood three trees that seemed rooted in bare rock. They rose tall and broad like thick-limbed oaks, their leaves a perfect golden hue, almost glowing in the light. The golden leaves rippled as though shaking in a breeze, but Jessica had an odd feeling that no wind blew over the island, that the trees might be moving entirely on their own.

The boat slid forward, the gap closed, the sight was lost. In the last moment Jessica heard a sound, a shiver of music like a chorus of flutes, high and pure and lonely. Before it faded, she felt a twist in her chest—it seemed to her the music was coming from the three trees. It was almost as though they were singing.

Mitch made a noise beside her—he was staring out with both hands gripping the rail of the boat. Katie had put a hand on his shoulder as though afraid he might jump overboard. "That's so great. It's so great," he said.

"It surely is," Katie said.

"Can't we go there, sir, please?" Mitch said. "Just to see it, just for a while?"

Hunter gave a sad shake of his head. "No, we must not."

"Is there a reason, then?" Katie said. "Are we forbidden?"

"Not as you mean it," he said as he slid the pole through the water. "Better to say that there are beauties a soul cannot bear when it isn't whole. To take you there, then take you away again...it would be too cruel. It would break your heart."

The boat moved ahead length by length. Jessica kept her eyes on the light behind them, hoping for another gap, even as the glow dwindled into the haze and the scent of the island was lost in the wet smell of the lake. When she finally looked away, she heard Mitch speak quietly.

"I really wanted to go there," he said.

And Mr. McNulty said, "Yes. So did I."

No one spoke after that. Hunter guided them across an open patch of lake where the splashing of the pole seemed the only sound in the world. Jessica watched the water ahead, feeling tired and empty. As marvelous as the place had been, she'd seen enough of it; she only wanted the journey to end, even if she wasn't ready for what came next. They rode out into a part of the lake where the trees grew widely spaced, with just two more ranks ahead of them. Beyond that lay open water, and beyond the water a shadow rose from the lake, a shadow like a dark curtain eighty feet tall.

It was a second barrier wall, but a barrier made of stone, a long saw-toothed ridge of fissured rock that ran off to the left and right. Tumbled boulders littered the water at the base, and along the ridgetop stunted trees had sprouted from cracks and hollows, dark-needled things with bent trunks and crooked limbs.

Hunter turned the boat towards a crevasse that clove the ridge from top to bottom. It offered a rocky passage into the ridge, a channel three times as wide as the boat. Looking ahead Jessica wasn't surprised to find that the way was blocked: two slabs of stone stood side-by-side in the channel with a sliver of light between them. Close by the stones rose another dark pillar, carved with odd signs and banded this time with metal hoops. When the boat slid near it, Mitch took hold of an iron ring near the waterline. "The second gate, sir?" he said.

"Just so," Hunter said. He struck the pillar three times, the deep chord thrumming in the air; the standing stones trembled but otherwise remained in place. Hunter struck the pillar twice more, the new tones blending with the echoes of the old. The stones shifted then with a reluctant shudder, swinging away as though on hinges, roiling the water and rocking the boat so that Mitch had to cling tightly to the ring. When the waters settled, Hunter poled them through the gate.

At the end of the passage they rode out into near-darkness. A damp fog hung low over the water, cold tatters drifting across them like the mists near the shore when they first arrived. Jessica tried to peer ahead but couldn't see much further than the light of the lantern.

The ride felt more unwieldy here than it had been earlier: odd currents rocked the boat and small eddies swirled and vanished for no obvious reason. Jessica wrapped her arms across her chest with her hands in her armpits, trying to keep the cold from seeping in. Worse than the cold was a strange heaviness, a sinking weight below her heart like a feeling of dread. It had knotted her stomach and seemed to be draining the strength from her arms. She stamped her feet and shivered with her teeth clenched.

She noticed Katie watching her, her face pale and drawn. "I'm sorry, Jessica, I truly am," Katie said. "We haven't helped you at all."

Jessica shook her head. "That's not true. You came with me, you've helped a lot."

"It's not enough. Only I don't know what else to do. I feel like I hardly understand anything right now."

"Same here," Mr. McNulty said.

"Like everything we knew is turned upside down. Or I've never really known much of anything about anything."

"Ahh—maybe," Mr. McNulty said. "But think about all the times you said to me, 'George, you old mule, the world's bigger than you think it is.' See there? You were right all along."

Katie's mouth twitched, like a half-smile. "Well. Not quite what I had in mind."

He straightened his glasses. "And there's this. Alex and his oddball ideas. You remember?"

Katie nodded. "I thought about that too."

"Heaven and hell. Maybe not so nutty after all."

They were starting to lose Jessica. She coughed and said, "Sorry—what's that about? If it's all right."

Ahead of them the lake water churned and Hunter drove the pole down to keep the boat steady. Whether for that or for some other reason Katie looked uncomfortable again. "Oh, Jessica, we shouldn't be bothering you—it's just something we heard a while back...."

Jessica didn't really care what they said, she just wanted them to keep talking. "It won't bother me. Go on. Please."

The waters calmed themselves and Hunter began poling again. Katie said, "Well, it's just this. An old friend of ours, Alex, had spent some time thinking about heaven and hell. And he told us this idea."

Mr. McNulty said, "He figured that in the end, we get to make a choice."

"Yes. He said—if I have it right—he said if you want heaven, you have to know it's a place where everything about you is remembered. And that means every single thing, even the awful secrets you've been hiding all your life. It's all known and remembered, and it's all forgiven, completely forgiven, every bit of it. Like the shame gets swallowed up in something bigger and no one bothers about it anymore."

Out beyond the prow of the boat the drifts of fog began

breaking apart, but Katie couldn't see them from where she sat. "But maybe you don't want that, Alex said; you don't want the truth about you to be so open. Or maybe you don't even want to know it yourself. If you're serious, you have another choice. You can hide, you can be lost—you can choose hell. Because in hell, nothing is known or remembered. So nothing can be forgiven."

As Katie finished speaking, a towering darkness seemed to emerge from the mists ahead. Jessica blinked and stared and the darkness took on a form. It looked rough-faced and steep-walled like the side of a cliff, except that a section had fallen away and an open space lay beyond it. Then she looked near the waterline, where huge roots sank gray and mildewed into the lake, and she realized with a start that they were approaching a stump, the broken remains of a tree that had been just as enormous as the world-trees in the lake behind them. Long ago the core must have hollowed out and a corner collapsed, leaving a gap through the walls, a narrow strait into a dark crater.

Hunter steered the boat towards the gap. They rode through disturbed waters, currents that ground the boat across broken roots and strips of bark. At the opening, Hunter heaved against the pole, driving them through the strait and out into a rough-edged pool, a pond that filled the base of the stump like water at the bottom of a bowl. Around the pool slabs of decayed heartwood staggered away from the water and the air seemed thickened by the smell of rot.

Rising in the center of the pool was a single standing stone: a gray weathered rock with no signs of working by any hands, except that rough iron bars had been set into its face like rungs of a ladder leading down to the water. Close by the stone stood another dark wooden pillar, banded with metal strips like the last one, but no carvings marked its surface. Instead, the wood looked cracked and grooved and the pillar leaned slightly to one side as though it had been standing in the water too long. Near the waterline was another iron ring; Mitch took hold of it when the boat slid close. "The third gate, sir?" he said.

"Yes. But it's a bit different than the others," Hunter said. He laid the pole inside the boat and braced his feet, leaning one hand against the pillar. Jessica noticed something then: one of the metal bands had a sharp point of metal, like the end of a nail or a spike about an inch long. She had begun to wonder why it was there when Hunter brought back his free hand and slapped it hard against the point. Jessica cringed and Hunter uttered a groan that seemed to tremble through the wood of the boat. He pulled his hand away and snapped it towards the face of the stone. A spray of drops spattered across the rock, deep red against the dull gray; as Jessica stared, she saw that they crossed over another scattering of spots, thin and faded like an ancient memory.

A current shifted the boat. At the base of the stone, below the last visible rung, the water spun into an eddy. The eddy quickened and widened like water running down a drain except that the eye seemed to be opening too fast. Before long the eye was a foot wide and still growing, spreading out as it brushed against the rock. When it reached about three feet across, it slowed and stopped and the waters around it slowed their circling. A hole had opened in the water beside the stone, with wet rungs leading downward out of sight.

Jessica stared at the hole without moving. She knew what came next but she wasn't sure her legs would do what they needed to do. They had gone numb from the cold and the heaviness in her chest, and she could hardly feel them when she rubbed her hands on her jeans.

She heard a sound beside her; she turned to see Hunter crouching on one knee. The creases around his eyes had deepened as though from pain or concern. "You're afraid," he said.

It was a relief to admit it. "Yes...very much." She nodded at the cloth he'd wrapped around his hand. "It really must've hurt. Will you be all right?"

He shrugged. "I've had worse." He leaned his head to one side. "Shall I take you back? It's not too late."

She sighed and shook her head. "No. Thanks. I have to do this. Even if it's stupid." He didn't smile, exactly, but she thought she saw an understanding in his eyes, or a kind of acceptance. Like a father's look, she thought. She would have liked to spend a long time looking at those eyes.

Hunter said, "I have one thing to give you," as he reached into a pocket of his coat. He drew out an object and placed it in her hand: a small white stone, rounded and smooth like a pebble from a streambed. It felt warm from his heat and sat comfortably in the middle of her palm.

"Take it as a reminder," he said. "It won't change what you have to do or make it simpler. But it may bring some things to mind." He closed a large hand over hers and she felt the warmth of it along the length of her arm.

Jessica met his eyes again. "The way you enter is the way you return," he said. "Remember that. Remember it even if everything else is lost."

She drew a long breath; the warmth seemed to have spread through her blood, all the way to her toes. "I will, sir, or I'll do my best. Thank you, for everything."

She placed the stone in her jacket pocket as she stood up. Mitch looked wretched, as miserable as she'd ever seen him; on an impulse she leaned over and hugged him, and he returned it, though it was awkward. She took Katie's hand and Mr. McNulty's hand for a moment—they said, "Please be safe," and "Come back to us," and she said "I will." With Hunter's help she stepped up on the rail of the boat and leaned over to take hold of the rungs. They chilled her skin but she held tight and swung her legs over, getting a good grip with her shoes.

"When you reach the end, let go," Hunter said. "You'll not be harmed."

She climbed down easily enough even though the rungs that had been underwater were slimy from the damp. Just a few feet below the waterline she reached down with a foot and couldn't find anywhere to put it. She took a breath and tried to release the rungs, but her hands wouldn't cooperate. Closing her eyes she thought about Ariel, and she let go. She felt herself falling then, quickly but not too quickly, sinking like a stone, down and down and down into the dark.

Chapter 10

The Country Where All Is Forgotten

SOME TIME after she'd let go of the rungs, and some while after the light above her had dwindled and vanished, Jessica couldn't tell whether she was still falling. She felt no rush of air or other sense of movement, nothing to see or touch. She seemed suspended, floating in a fog or some other sort of gray space. If she was traveling from one place to another, it felt very different than it ever had before. Now and then she stretched out her hands and feet, hoping to reach something solid, and she tried to be patient since there didn't seem much else to do.

On the fourth or fifth stretch one of her shoes bumped against a surface, and without any other effort both feet settled onto firm ground. She released a long breath, glad to feel her own weight again. Through the fog, she checked the surface under her feet—it felt harder than bare earth but not quite like stone. As a guess, she would have said it was cracked concrete. She scuffed it with a shoe and it even felt like concrete.

Weird, she thought. In front of her the fog seemed to be thinning. She took a step forward and then another, and when the mist rolled away behind her she came to a halt.

She stood, as far as she could tell, in the middle of a narrow street. The pavement, cracked and slightly damp, curved to the left not far ahead. Along both sides tall gray houses or other buildings stood shoulder-to-shoulder, and above the rooftops a flat overcast drifted across the sky. The air tasted stale and there was no sound.

Jessica waited, absolutely still. Nothing moved except a thin mist drifting along the sidewalks. She scanned the buildings on either side; they all seemed real enough but looked ragged and worn, with cracked walls and shuttered windows and eaves that sagged over the street. The few uncovered windows opened into dark spaces that appeared empty from where she stood. It all felt thoroughly deserted.

"Okay," she said under her breath. "Not what I expected." But then, what *had* she expected? Monstrous guards or a great iron gate? Well, something like that—certainly not a run-down alley in an abandoned city. She turned her head far enough to look back over her shoulder. The fog or mist still lay behind her, a faint barrier drifting upward like fine smoke. It looked nothing like a gate, but if it brought her in then it must also be the way out. Whatever else happened she had to find her way back to that spot.

With her hands in her jacket pockets, she took a few cautious steps, cringing at the noise of her footfalls. Some of the nearby buildings had dark entrances at ground level, their doors standing open or sagging off their hinges. She wondered if she'd have to search those rooms, stepping through doorways one by one to see what lay inside; she shuddered and kept walking. Best not to take chances yet—she might learn more as she went further.

Around the left-hand bend the street continued unchanged. She kept walking as the street made a second bend and then a sharp turn to the right. Here the lane opened out into an intersection or crossroads, with six or seven streets twisting off in various directions. They all looked identical, lined with ragged

gray buildings and sidewalks adrift in fog. She could see no
signs or landmarks to tell her where she was or where she was
going.

She stood in the intersection trying not to feel overwhelmed. "Quit moping," she muttered. "I'm not giving up. So
how do I keep from getting lost?"

She might have made a map if she'd brought the right tools;
but she had no pens or pencils, and no paper for that matter.
Great planning, she thought. *Well, maybe I could leave a trail as I
go. Only I didn't bring breadcrumbs either.* She patted her jacket
and jeans, looking for loose items that could be dropped on the
ground. In a pants pocket she found some flat round objects
she didn't recognize and pulled one out.

It was a bright yellow button with a slogan on it, one of the
pins that people had been handing out at Esterhaus for Aspiration Day. The slogan read "I'M THE BEST, AND SO ARE YOU!" in
large letters. She felt a shock of surprise: *When did that happen
—days ago? No, just hours. It was only this morning.* She flipped
the button in her hand, then shrugged as she bent down. She
placed it face down on the pavement with the pin pointing to
the street she had come from, the street that led the way home.

She said, "I guess, as long it as stays there—" but didn't
complete the thought. From the corner of an eye, she saw
someone walking towards her.

She turned with a stiff neck. A man, a tall man, had stepped
from a sidewalk into the intersection—and he was entirely gray.
From his shoes and clothes to his hands and face and hair he
was the color of ash, the color of smoke, and it seemed to
Jessica that his edges were slightly blurred, like a photo not
quite in focus. He walked in her direction without making a
sound.

Her muscles had pulled so tight she could not have moved
even if she'd known where to go. The man drew close enough
for her to see the grimness in his face, eyes narrowed and

staring ahead, brows wrinkled and lips pressed shut. If he had stopped beside her or turned to face her, she might have completely panicked—but he did not. He walked past not more than two feet away, still silent, never slowing or glancing in her direction.

Jessica had never felt so grateful to be ignored. She allowed herself to relax as the man stepped from the pavement to another misty sidewalk. She began to wonder if others like him might be nearby; but then she blinked twice and the world shifted. She saw what she hadn't seen or hadn't wanted to see until then: the fog along the sidewalk wasn't fog but people, a flowing crowd of people, all of them shadowy and blurred like the gray man. Jessica jerked her head towards the other streets and they were all the same. The shadow-people walked along every sidewalk, as gray and colorless as the buildings and the air.

Her legs wanted to take her back the way she'd come but she held them still. She forced herself to pay attention, watching people on the sidewalks nearby. None of them bothered to look at her; like the gray man they all stared ahead, ignoring the girl with the bright orange jacket standing in the middle of the intersection. *They don't care about me*, she told herself. *They don't care about me and they're not going to hurt me. It's okay. I can keep going.*

She took a few stiff steps, and then a few more, moving into one of the branching streets. After a dozen yards she looked back again. The button still lay untouched and unnoticed in the middle of the crossroads, but as a marker for the way home it seemed much too vulnerable.

"Got to find Ariel," she said under her breath. "I've got to find her and get us out of here, fast."

She continued down the middle of the street with her shoulders hunched as though it might make her less conspicuous. Along the sidewalks the gray people flowed in constant streams like walkers on a crowded day in a big city. They all seemed intent on some purpose, though Jessica couldn't see anywhere for them to go; and she thought it odd that they kept to the sidewalks while the streets were so empty. And something else seemed equally odd. A few buildings had glass windows at street level and she could see reflections of people in those windows, but whenever she looked at them, they didn't match the people on the sidewalk. Some of the reflections faced away from the street while others stared outward without moving, as though they had no connection with the people passing by.

She had almost passed through the next intersection before remembering to mark the trail. Gritting her teeth, she hurried back to the street she had come from, pulling out a button and placing it where the street met the intersection. *That's better than pointing with the pin*, she thought; *when I come back, I'll just take the street with the button.* She continued through the crossroads, taking a lane that looked wider than the others, moving faster now. In the back of her mind she felt—or hoped—that the place couldn't be just an endless confusion of streets. There had to be a center or a vantage point where it made some kind of sense, and if she could find that place it might give her a way to find Ariel.

More walking, the derelict buildings passing in an irregular blur. A few more intersections, all of them carefully marked. She tried to choose the larger streets but she began to think it didn't make much difference—they all looked more or less the same once she was in them. She felt fatigue creeping up her legs, just as the street she was following took a bend to the right and ended at a broad open space. The trail-marking had become such a habit by then that she put down a button before taking a good look.

It looked like a kind of plaza or a town square. Around the edges at least a dozen streets led away, none of them looking much different than the others. In the center stood a cracked mass of stone that might have been a ruined fountain, as dry as old bones. Aside from some shadow-people crossing with long strides the place was empty.

Could this be the center? It wasn't quite what she'd hoped for—but she had no guarantee there'd be anything better farther on. "If I'm going to try something it might as well be here," she muttered. She walked out to the middle, stopping at one point to let shadow-people pass. A crumbled stone wall a couple of feet high surrounded the dry fountain, and she climbed up on it, facing out over the plaza. She took a long breath and called out:

"*Ariel!...Ariel!...Ariel, it's Jessica!...Can you hear me?...Ariel!... Are you out there?...Ariel, come and find me!...Ariel!...Ariel!....*"

Echoes returned to her and she took that as a good sign: her voice might be carrying farther than she expected. She kept calling as loud as she could manage without straining her voice. Before long there came a response, but not the one she'd hoped for: all around the plaza shadow-people began slowing their strides and turning to the sound of her voice. Jessica's hands felt clammy but she didn't stop, not when she felt the many eyes on her from every side, not even when the gray forms started to drift in her direction. One by one they crossed the space in silence and gathered in front of the wall where she stood.

"*Ariel!...Ariel!...Ariel, are you there?....*" There were scores of them now, all gray and grim-faced, staring up at her with unchanging expressions. Jessica tried not to meet their eyes but she couldn't help noticing the faces: many kinds of people, men and women, some older and some younger—"so many stories," as Katie had said. Jessica wondered if their stories might be as different as their faces, or if they would have sounded much the same; she wondered what had brought them there and whether they would always stay; she wondered if they could tell her if she asked.

She kept calling, and as she called, she rummaged through memories, trying to see whether she'd started to forget things as Hunter had warned. Nothing was missing as far as she could tell. *But how would I know when I've forgotten something?* she thought. *If I lose memories, how can I tell they're gone? Maybe they would disappear like they were never there. Maybe I've forgotten stuff already and don't know it.* She tightened her fists and tried to call louder.

By now, the crowd filled most of the plaza and people still drifted in from the streets. Jessica's voice had gone raspy and doubts had crept in: this was taking too long—Ariel was too far away—she would never find her in time. She felt a growing certainty that the calling wasn't going to work no matter how hard she tried. She just couldn't reach far enough with her voice.

But with that thought she remembered the hail she had sent to Mr. Peabody. She stopped calling when the idea struck her: *Could I do that here? Would Ariel hear it?* She brought up the shape, the long sweeping curve like a soaring bird, and as soon as she saw it clearly she slipped Ariel's name into it and let it go.

"....aaaaaaAAAAAAARRRRRRRRIIIIIIIIIEEEEEEELLLLLLL-LLLLLllllllll...."

Something happened as it left her, a thing barely visible, like a ripple or a shudder that moved out through the plaza and the streets. *Whoa...I don't think that happened last time.* After a moment's rest she sent the hail again, and then again. It took more out of her than she expected—she felt light-headed and her legs began to sway. She breathed deeper, working up the strength to make the effort several more times if she had to.

Then at the edge of the plaza, moving out from one of the

streets, Jessica saw a figure that looked smaller than most of the shadow-people. It was too far away to see clearly but she thought its face and clothes carried a hint of color. She stepped down from the wall and worked her way forward, murmuring "...excuse me...sorry...excuse me..." as she went. No one stood in her way. Now that she had gone quiet the shadow-people began drifting apart and drifting away until she had space enough to pass.

The figure was Ariel—Jessica knew it before she reached the edge of the square; but her rush of relief vanished quickly. Of all the things she had seen until then, nothing had been more frightening than the sight of Ariel's face. She stared straight ahead, her skin pale and nearly gray, her forehead wrinkled and her eyes narrowed and her lips pressed shut. She looked so much like the shadow-people that Jessica couldn't be sure she was still alive.

"Ariel?" she said. "Ariel, are—are you there?"

No response, no glimmer of recognition. Biting a lip, Jessica came close and took Ariel's hand; it felt deeply cold, but with a slow pulse beneath the skin. She squeezed hard and said, "Ariel, it's me. It's Jessica. Can you hear me?"

The girl shivered and her eyes partly focused. "Uh..." she said. "Jess...umm...Jessica?"

"Yes. It's me."

"Uh...." She blinked twice. "You came. You found me."

A new flood of relief, stronger this time. "Yes. I came because you called me. You remember that?"

"Umm...oh." Her voice slow and vague, as though speaking from a half-sleep. "Umm... I guess so. I don't...it's, uh, hard to remember."

"Yeah, I heard about that. It's okay now. You'll be all right once we're out of here—I hope. We're going to leave. Can you walk with me?"

"Oh. Sure." Jessica kept hold of her hand, pulling her toward the street she had marked with a button. Ariel's steps were nearly as sluggish as her voice. "It's good you came," she said.

"Yeah. I'm really glad I found you."

"I could, umm...couldn't get out, by myself. I tried. A long time ago. But I forgot, umm...I forgot my music."

"Yeah, I'm sure."

"So...so I waited. I stayed near your brother and watched the people. There wasn't anywhere to go, you know...."

"Wait," Jessica said. She squeezed Ariel's hand tight. "My brother? You found Brad? He's here?"

"Uh-huh...well, sort of."

"*Sort of?* What do you mean?"

She could have counted off the seconds while Ariel's thoughts came together. "It's, umm...it's like he's...it's hard to explain, I guess. You want to see?"

Jessica looked to the street where the button lay waiting. If they went that way right now, if they only followed the trail, she knew they could find the way out without any trouble. It was the simple thing to do, even the smart thing to do. "You can take me to him? You're sure?" she said.

"Umm...yeah. Sure."

Jessica let out a breath through her teeth. "Let's go there, but we have to hurry—I mean *really* hurry."

"Yeah, okay." Ariel looked around the square. "What street did I come from?"

Jessica pointed to it and they began to walk. Ariel moved and spoke more easily now and Jessica listened without really hearing what she said. She tried not to think too much or imagine what they were going to find. She'd told Mitch that she had to know if Brad was there and she meant it when she said it. But Brad as a smoke-thing, wandering grim-faced along those streets—maybe that was more than she wanted to know and much more than she wanted to see.

The route they followed took a few turns and Ariel became

tentative, looking around as though nearly lost. Then she pulled up short and said "Oh—this way," turning into a narrow passage or alley between two larger streets. The buildings there had windows but no doorways that Jessica could see, and no shadow-people were walking nearby. Halfway down the alley Ariel stopped and sighed as though she wasn't planning to go further.

"What are you doing?" Jessica said. "There's no one here."

"Not in the street," Ariel said. "In the window."

Jessica turned to the window and almost jerked back. There was a reflection in the glass, and like other reflections in that place it didn't match the surroundings. It showed a dank-looking room or a corner of a vacant house, with sheets covering a window and wallpaper peeling in strips. A young man in stained clothing sprawled across an old mattress on the floor. His hair looked stringy and damp and he lay with his head thrown back as though snoring, but Jessica guessed he was drunk or stoned. She couldn't be sure about him until his head turned and his nose twitched in a familiar way. "Oh no, oh no," she said. "It's Brad—it's really Brad. You found him."

"Uh-huh."

"He looks so terrible," she said. "But where is he? Why is he in the window? Is he in the building?"

"Umm...no. He's...umm...." Waiting through the pauses had become painful. "People in the windows, they're not...not really here."

"What? Not in Oblivion?"

"Yeah...it's like...like they're *partway* here. Or they *feel* like they're here. Or they're sort of on their way, maybe. That's why we see them. You see?"

"Uh, no. But you mean, he's still alive right now?"

"Yeah. Right now."

"Then where is he really? Or where is that room?"

"Umm...I can't tell from here. Sorry."

In the window, Brad's arm twitched and his nose wrinkled again. It seemed crazy that she'd come so far only to find he was no closer than he'd ever been. She rocked on her toes and said, "Well, there's got to be...look, if we can see him, can he see us too? Or can he hear us, even?"

"Uh...I don't think so. But I don't know."

Brad's eyelids flickered as though he might be waking up. Jessica stepped closer to the window. "Brad!" she called. "It's me! It's Jessica! Can you hear me?" No response as far as she could see. She raised her voice. "Brad, I'm here! I can see you! I want to help! Listen to me, please!"

A stirring in the reflection: Brad shook his head and looked here and there in the room. Jessica drew up her strength and called again, trying to force the words through the glass. "Brad, you don't have to be there! I don't care what the trouble is. We want to help you, I know we can help you!"

Brad lost some of his bleariness and his gaze no longer wandered—he seemed to stare directly out of the window. Jessica called, "Brad, if you can hear me at all, don't stay there! Get away and come home! Come home, so we can help you! It doesn't matter what's happened! I love you! Mom loves you! She wants to see you again, really bad! Please come home, please!" Brad raised up on one elbow, his eyes widened and his lips moving as though he were speaking. Then in a single moment the reflection trembled and vanished, wiping away and leaving nothing but bare glass.

Jessica leaned her head against the wall, thoroughly spent. "Well, that was pointless," she muttered. Brad was alive, at least, but she still had no idea how to find him or make things better. All that effort and she'd come back to where she started....

She blinked a few times. In a drowsy sort of way, she realized she'd been standing and staring at nothing. The buildings nearby seemed unfamiliar even though they'd walked into the alley a few minutes before. "Ariel," she said, "umm...which way did we come in here?"

Ariel wrinkled her nose. "Oh...not sure. Why?"

Jessica stared at her. "Why? It's *important*. Because—because...." For a long, blank, sickening moment she couldn't say why it mattered. She stamped a foot and said, "It's because...*we have to go back the way I came.*" She almost panted with the effort. "I left a—a trail, on the way in here. You understand?"

"Umm...maybe."

"Ariel...." There were things she had to say but the words wouldn't come together; every movement in her head felt like wading through mud. She squeezed her fists tighter. "Ariel, listen. It's happening, I'm forgetting stuff, and we have to get out of here. You've got to take me back to...to the place where we met. The open place. The—the *plaza*. You understand? If we get back there, we can follow the trail but we have to go *right now*."

The urgency didn't seem to register. "Okay," Ariel said, looking around the alleyway. "Uh...I think it was this way. Come on."

It wasn't the direction Jessica would have picked. When they came to the wider street Jessica would have turned right but Ariel turned left. Jessica didn't argue—she couldn't feel certain about anything now, she didn't recognize the buildings and the street twisted in directions she didn't remember. For all she knew their path might have been random.

Just ahead of her Ariel came to a halt, for no reason she could see. "Umm, Jessica...we're here."

She was right: in front of them the street emptied into a wide square, the plaza with the ruined fountain. "Ariel—that's great. So now...now...." Confusion again: why had they come here? Off to the left something lay at the edge of a street, a small round object on the pavement. "There! That's the trail. Come on, this way."

They ran to the marked street and Jessica picked up the button. She saw at once that it had changed, the colors now faded and pale as though they had somehow drained away; and the arm of her orange jacket seemed to have faded too, like cloth left too long in the sun. "Oh, Ariel, it's getting worse" she said. "But we just follow the buttons, okay? If we do that I think we can make it."

They ran down the twisting street that Jessica felt she'd never seen before, running as fast as they could though it never seemed fast enough. Deep in her head Jessica could feel the blankness, the forgetting, rising like water, flowing through her past like a dark tide. Her memories seemed to sink in it, drowning quietly except for a few that struggled at the end. A neighbor's puppy shivering nervously at the top of a backyard slide; a bright yellow rose with a scent like ripe oranges; Mitch's eyes, black and blue from a lump on his forehead; a desk she'd sat in at school, with the name *Roscoe* carved along one edge; her mother's tired smile. One by one they flared in her mind and vanished, dying like embers in a fireplace. "Ariel," she said, panting, "I can feel it. It's all going away."

"I know."

"Little pieces of me. I'm losing them. I'm crumbling inside."

"I know. I'm sorry."

As bad as it was, they still had the trail: at every crossroads they found a street with a faded button, and she never had to think, she just picked them up and kept going. Several of them jangled in her pocket now and she knew the end couldn't be much farther. But the streets kept twisting and twisting and the gray buildings went by like they'd never end....

There, just ahead: a wide intersection with several streets leading away. "Ariel, come on, we might be close," she said. They ran out from the street and stopped as Jessica picked up the button that lay in the center, and when Ariel caught her breath she said, "Where do we go? The streets aren't marked here."

Jessica looked at the button, turning it over in her hand. "Oh," she said.

"What?"

A vague uncertainty stirred in her head. "Ariel, I think... maybe this button was different."

"Oh?"

"It was upside-down...out in the middle. I think maybe... umm, the pin pointed the way we should go."

"Yeah? Where was it pointing?"

Jessica looked around them. "I didn't...I didn't notice," she said.

"Oh."

Jessica stood there as her heart slowed and her breath calmed. It seemed to her, distantly, that she ought to feel anxious or upset about what had happened. But she didn't, really. She didn't feel much of anything at all.

All around them people kept walking as though they knew where they were going. Ariel said, "So...what should we do?"

Jessica shook her head. "I'm not sure. I can't, umm...my head just feels numb."

"Yeah."

"But...the street behind us. Is that the one we came from?"

"Uh...I think so."

"Then maybe we could take the street straight ahead. And see what happens."

"Yeah. Okay."

They followed the street quietly in the silence. Jessica didn't recognize anything but she didn't expect to. The buildings looked like all the other buildings and the gray people flowed like mist along the sidewalks. It felt good not to be hurrying anymore.

She put her hands in her jacket as they walked. In the right-hand pocket something round and smooth brushed her fingers —the white stone. When her hand closed on it the voice came back to her, as clearly as if the man were speaking beside her: *The way you enter is the way you return. Remember that.* She weighed the words and shook her head. "It's no good," she muttered. "I don't have the way anymore. It's just too late."

They passed through a few intersections (three? four? she wasn't sure), until the street ended at an open space, a wide square with other streets leading away. In the center stood the ruins of a stone fountain. "Is this...are we at the same place, where we were before?" Jessica said.

"Umm...I don't know," Ariel said. "I think maybe there're lots of places like this—I sort of remember that. Lots of plazas. And they all look the same."

"Oh...I thought there was...only one."

They stood for a time since there didn't seem anything better to do, then sat on the crumbling wall around the ruined fountain. Above the rooftops the overcast dragged across the sky as it always had. They sat and watched the gray people as they walked by, always walking, crossing from one side to the other.

In the slow movements of Jessica's mind one of the shadows felt darker than the rest. She tried to find a way to speak it aloud.

"Ariel...I'm so sorry. I messed it all up," she said.

"Oh?"

"I failed you." The words felt dry in her mouth. "I wanted to get you away from here. Now we're both lost. I made everything worse."

"But you tried. You tried really hard."

She shrugged at that. "You know, I can't even picture anything—from outside, anymore. Or if I think of something it's all...all fuzzy. Like I only imagined it."

"Yeah. Like this is the only place there is. The only *real* place."

"Yeah. Like that."

"We can't get out 'cause there's nowhere to go."

Still later Ariel said, "It's not so bad. Forgetting stuff, I mean."

"Oh?"

"It's easier, I guess. I don't think I liked remembering stuff. Maybe it used to hurt. I don't know why. It's better when it doesn't hurt."

"Yeah."

Even later Ariel said, "It's funny, when the color starts leaving your eyes. You can kind of feel it when it goes."

Jessica looked up at the ragged sky. She knew they wouldn't sit there much longer, they would start walking again. They would walk and keep walking because everyone there always walked. They would wander the gray streets and maybe after a time they would move to the sidewalks with everyone else, two more faces among all the rest. They would stop speaking because they had nothing to say and they would stare straight ahead because there was nothing to see. And maybe they would hardly notice when their faces turned grim and the last streaks of color drained away....

Ariel said, "So, should we start walking now?"

Jessica shook her head but stood up without meaning to do it. She didn't want to walk but her legs moved anyway, one stiff step after another. Ariel fell in alongside her, keeping pace. They headed for one of the streets that led away from the plaza, it didn't matter which one, it was all endless once you began—

Jessica caught her lip between her teeth and bit down; she jammed a heel hard into the pavement. "Wait," she grunted. "Just wait."

"Huh? Why?"

The pain in her foot sparked a flash of anger, narrow and fragile like a red thread. "It's not...we can't do this," she said. "Can't just give up. There's got to be...." She couldn't find an ending for the sentence. As she groped for words, she noticed something else: in her clenched fist in her pocket she still held the white stone.

She brought the stone out, letting it rest in her open palm. A disquiet tugged at the back of her mind, an unsettled feeling, as though she'd gone off and left something unfinished or incomplete.

Ariel said, "Jessica, what is it?"

Jessica shook her head again; she gripped the stone tight, trying to push through the fatigue. "Listen. A thing I still remember—it's not much but you should hear it. There was a man, on the outside, who helped me before I came here. He told me how to get out after I found you. He said, 'The way you enter is the way you return.'"

"Oh. What did he mean?"

"I thought...we had to go back to the spot, where I came in. That's why I made the, umm...the trail, you know? But, umm...." She gripped the stone tighter. "But I'm not sure anymore. Maybe he meant something different, like...like *how* I got in here, *how* it happened. You see? Maybe we were supposed to do the same thing, to get back out."

"Oh. Does that help?"

"Well...." With eyes shut she strained to bring back an image she could grasp. "I can't...I can't picture what happened. It's blank like everything else. It's too late. It doesn't do us any good."

Opening her eyes, she found Ariel watching her intently. "Maybe...well, maybe I could make you see him," she said.

"What?"

"The guy who talked to you. I could try to make you see him, in your head."

"But you...you forgot your music."

"Yeah, but this is different. It's about you, not me." Her eyes narrowed. "I can feel it inside you. It's hiding but it's not gone. It just has to come out. Only...umm, it won't be easy. I mean, it might even hurt. It might hurt you or it might hurt me."

Jessica hardly heard what Ariel was saying. The last of her strength had ebbed and she could feel the dark tide in her head again, rising and rising, ready to swallow her whole. With her jaw tight she said, "Ariel, it doesn't matter, in a few minutes we'll forget everything we talked about, we'll be stuck here for good. If you can do anything just do it, just do it *right now*."

Ariel stood with her eyes raised for a long moment as though unwilling to move; then she brought up her pipes and blew into them to clear them. She knelt on the pavement, rocking slightly on her bare knees, curling tight like a ball. She drew a deep breath and arched back and let out a yell—a long cry of pain or release, rising in pitch until it reached a single pure tone. She held it until the cords stood out in her neck and Jessica thought she must collapse or faint; then she cut it off and began to play.

The tones were hardly in the air before Jessica said "Uhhh..." as her breath left her. In that gray place the music seemed the most marvelous sound she'd ever heard. The notes soared and reveled, climbing like startled birds in the pale air and echoing like an anthem from a choir. Under Jessica's feet the ground trembled like a sounding board and all around the square shadow-people halted and turned to the music, their faces almost softening. And then all of it vanished.

She was sitting on a wooden bench in a boat that rocked

lightly beneath her; nearby rose a gray stone studded with iron rungs that led into a hole in the water. She turned to her right and Hunter was there, crouching on one knee, his face so vivid she could see scars on his cheeks and fine hairs in his beard, and when she breathed, she inhaled a cedar scent from his woolen coat. His eyes held a knowing look, knowing and kindly, but darkened with a shadow of pain. He lifted his arm, and when Jessica looked down she saw that his hand was closed, with bright red blood leaking between his fingers.

The image fled, the gray world returned. Jessica gasped, "Ariel, I saw him! You did it! I was in a boat and...and Hunter opened the gate. That's how I got here. The way I entered—he opened the gate. And to do it he—he had to...oh, Ariel, he wounded himself—"

If she stopped to think she might lose her nerve. She reached into her pocket, grabbed one of the trail-marking buttons, popped open the pin with her thumb, and jammed the point into her other palm.

A burst of fire in her hand and arm, spiking up her shoulder into her head; she gave an aching groan that shuddered up from her gut. She pulled out the pin and through the haze in her eyes watched the blood well up from the wound and run down to hang at the edge of her palm. It seemed thin to her, thin and weak, a pale reflection of the real substance; but it was enough, more than enough in that insubstantial place. The blood hung from her palm but did not fall. She felt her arm begin to rise, her whole body lifting of its own accord, until the soles of her shoes barely gripped the pavement.

"*Ariel, grab my hand!*" she yelled, as around her all the shades of gray began to swirl like water.

Chapter 11

Nothing Quite the Same

SHE FLOUNDERED IN WATER, trying to keep her head up, confused because the water didn't feel very wet and she could breathe, most of the time, without much trouble. She held onto a hand she thought was her friend's and tried to move upward, though it often felt more like sideways or backwards or staying in one place. But the confusion didn't last. Strong arms wrapped around her, someone took hold of her free hand. She felt herself lifting, rising out of the water; she heard voices beside her: "...it's all right...got you...oh my goodness...you're safe, both of you."

She sat in a boat that slipped quietly across a misted lake. She felt the bench rock beneath her and watched ripples fan away over the dark waters. The boat held a few other people, a boy and a man and woman; the woman sat next to her pressing a cloth against her hand. Ariel sat on the other side, chattering like she'd known these people all her life, stopping only to hug Jessica and say "You *saved* me! You *saved* me!" and squeezing so hard it felt like her ribs would crack.

The boy sat across from her, looking concerned. She would have said something to make him feel better if she'd known what the problem was. Then as she watched, his features shifted, settling into a face she knew almost as well as her own.

"Oh," she said, blinking. "Mitch."

"Well, hi," he said, eyebrows raised. "How you doing now?"

"Umm...better. Maybe."

"We've been worried. You've been a total space cadet."

"Oh...yeah. That's about right." The older people in the boat were Katie and Mr. McNulty, of course. They had been listening to Ariel as she kept on talking. Katie still held Jessica's left hand, pressing on the makeshift bandage; the wound throbbed with a dull ache.

"Ariel's told us the story," Mitch said. "Guess she recovers quicker than you."

"Uh-huh...that's normal. But you guys, umm...you were waiting all that time?"

"Well, here's the crazy thing—okay, it's all been crazy, but still: it was really quick for us."

"What?"

"Seriously. You went down in the water and we talked for just a few minutes before Hunter was reaching down and pulling you out. Katie and Mr. McNulty helped with Ariel."

Jessica tried to absorb what he was saying. "No, no, that's not right. It was like...I don't know. Hours and hours. Or days."

"Yeah, we figured. Mr. McNulty said something must be different about that place. Or maybe it's this forest-lake, instead. Everything else here is funny, so it's almost consistent."

"I guess so." She didn't feel ready to think about anything that complicated.

Ariel had gone quiet, finally, and Katie gave Jessica's hand a light squeeze. "Jessica, dear, I can't even begin to imagine what you've been through, and I'm so sorry, for both of you. To feel yourselves trapped in that terrible place...there just aren't any words. But it's marvelous that you've come all the way back to us. Really, you astound me."

"Yep," Mr. McNulty said, "that's the word for it."

"Ariel says you're a hero," Mitch said.

"Huh? Not even."

"Don't lie, you know it's true," Ariel said.

Jessica made a disgusted sound. "Now you're being silly. We did it together. Because you played the music, remember? And because I saw...."

Jessica looked towards the stern, where Hunter was steadily poling the boat. His eyes watched the water ahead and he'd turned up the collar of his coat against the cold and the fog. "Oh, sir—it was great, all that you did," she said. "It helped so much."

"She's right," Ariel said.

"We'd still be there—we'd be sitting in that plaza, or walking...." She broke off shivering as the memories flooded back. Hunter said, "That's enough, I think. And you're welcome, many times more than welcome."

Jessica had more to say but Katie spoke first. "Hunter, if it's all right," she said, "I hardly know the first thing about all this, of course, but listening to Ariel it was tragic to hear about all the others there, in Oblivion. Do you know what will happen to them?"

"Well, now," he said, "if you're wishing to learn the ends of all tales and the destiny of every soul—that may be more than I can give you."

"Oh. Of course. Then I suppose what I'm asking is, will Oblivion always be there?"

"To that I would say, certainly not," he said, switching sides with the pole. "And you may know that already. A day will come, as you may have heard, when all things change in all the worlds, and all themes and covenants find their proper ends. On that day even Oblivion will change and will not be what it was. But what follows that, I'm afraid, is more than I can say."

While Hunter was speaking, the air around the boat

seemed to brighten and the last shreds of fog slipped away. Ahead of them Jessica saw a shoreline with a wooded slope climbing into the misted air, and at the base of the nearest trees she could make out the first steps of a stone stairway. "Oh, that's —are we back where we started, already?" she said.

"You missed a lot on the way," Mitch said.

"Yeah, I guess. Then, sir, is that the way home?"

"Yes, for the four of you," Hunter said.

"Four...you mean, not Ariel?"

"Just so."

"Oh, that can't be right," she said, but looking at Ariel, she knew it was. The girl was grinding a toe on the planks and looking mournful.

"Sorry, Jessica," she said. "I'm gonna go be with Mr. Peabody for now."

"But why?"

"I know I made him worry when I went away. I bet he was *really* worried. I feel like I need to tell him I'm sorry, at least. Do you think that's right, Mr. Hunter?"

"I'd say so. And it's likely your guardian will provide a place for you to rest, to heal and learn and understand after all that's happened."

"But will that take long?" Jessica said. "She's not going away for good, is she?"

But Hunter had become preoccupied with guiding the boat as they neared the shore. He used the pole to swing the stern until the boat slid alongside the shingle at the water's edge, finally grating to a stop on a shelf below the waterline. He stepped ashore and helped Katie climb out along with Mr. McNulty. Before Mitch followed, he turned to Ariel.

"Okay, I gotta ask," he said. "Mr. Peabody told us you picked the name 'Ariel' after he found you."

"Yup."

"I've been wanting to know, why *that* name?"

"Oh, well...." She squinted, thinking about it. "It was kind of funny. He asked me my name and I didn't know, but one thing I remembered was this movie I saw when I was a kid. It was a cartoon movie about this girl who lives in the ocean, and she has a tail like a fish, except later she goes on land and gets real legs, but then she can't talk."

Mitch wrinkled his nose. "'The Little Mermaid'?"

"Yeah, that's it. Her name was Ariel, and I always liked the name, so I picked it. Did you see the movie? I liked it a lot."

Mitch turned to Mr. McNulty, who seemed preoccupied with adjusting his glasses. He cleared his throat and said, "So. The first rule of research."

"Never throw anything away," Mitch said automatically. "You're right. We had that and we threw it away. How dumb. We should've known better."

"One more thing we've learned today, I suppose."

Mitch got out then but Jessica didn't follow. She chewed the inside of her lip, feeling unsettled; the whole thing was happening too fast. "This really stinks," she said.

"Yeah," Ariel said.

"I just found you and now we have to say goodbye?"

"Uh-huh. But I don't think it'll be so long this time." Then almost shyly: "Friends forever?"

Jessica had to smile. "You bet."

"Don't forget about me, okay?"

"Like I could. But no more crazy stuff until you come back, okay?"

"Nope. Cross my heart."

When Jessica stepped onto the shore, Ariel said, "Oh, almost forgot, I have something for you." She dug into a pocket and brought out a small wrapped package. "I made you a present while I was away."

The wrapping looked crude, just wrinkled brown paper tied with a piece of string, but when Jessica touched it she somehow understood what was inside, and she knew exactly what it would do. She looked up, eyes widening. "Are you—are you sure?"

"Yup. No doubt. Later, alligator." Jessica stowed the gift in her jacket with a hand that shook just a bit.

She turned to Hunter, feeling she ought to say something more than just *goodbye*; but when she met his eyes and felt the warmth in them again, she knew she had no words for what she wanted to say. Before she began to stammer, he stopped her with a gesture: he held out his bandaged hand, the palm open. After a moment Jessica placed her own wounded hand in his, and he covered in gently with his other. Then he bent forward, almost like a bow, and spoke so only she could hear.

"Rest easy, daughter," he said. "You've done well. Very well indeed."

She mumbled a *thank you* and walked away in a half-daze, looking back only when she reached the others at the bottom of the stairway. She saw Hunter turn his face towards her and Ariel lift her arm to wave, just before the tree branches hid them from sight.

She sighed and began climbing with the others. For some reason the steps now felt taller or farther apart than when they descended—the sixth step much farther than the fifth, and the seventh farther still. On the next step, after Jessica raised her foot as high as she could reach, it took a long, long while to put it back down. When her foot finally landed she stumbled forward, blinking, into a cold wind under a night sky. They had already arrived outside the McNulty's back gate, at the spot where Mr. Peabody met them. The stars still shone brilliantly and the wind still gusted, sharp enough to cut through her clothes.

"Huh," Mitch said. "Welcome back."

Katie held a hand to her head to steady herself. "My goodness. So wonderful to be home," she said. "But it's not the same anymore, is it? Maybe nothing's quite the same after all that."

"Maybe not," Mr. McNulty said. "But at least there's coffee. Feels like I've been forever without it."

Jessica went home that night and slept a deep and quiet sleep. In the morning she awoke long enough to place a new bandage on the wound and tell her mother she wasn't feeling well. She went back to bed and slept through the afternoon, awaking near sunset to find that she felt, for the most part, all right.

Sort of. In a way.

The next morning, she made it to the bus stop just before the bus pulled away. She sat across the aisle from Mitch; he nodded to her with a wry expression, as though to say, *Back to normal. How weird is that?*

He spoke as the bus started moving. "Well, one thing's for sure."

"What's that?"

"School won't seem so bad anymore, after where you've been."

He was right, though not quite the way he meant it.

She felt different at Esterhaus that day and the days that followed—oddly detached or displaced, as though things around her weren't quite real and she only watched them from a distance. The worst of it passed after a few days but even afterwards she couldn't take problems as seriously as she used to. The gossip and insults at school just seemed childish and she couldn't tell why they had angered her so much a few weeks ago. One Friday at her Convergence Group, when Olivia LaRusso made a remark about "local kids who never learn to dress themselves," Jessica laughed like it was the silliest thing she'd ever heard. Olivia looked at her with a kind of shock, as though she'd never entirely noticed her before.

The wound in her left hand healed, leaving a pale scar in the middle of the palm. The hand throbbed or ached at odd moments, making her think that the pain might never entirely leave. In the past she would have resented that kind of thing but now she almost felt grateful: she took it as a memento of where she'd gone and what she'd done. Occasionally she touched the scar with a curled finger, knowing she could never really doubt what had happened or imagine it was some sort of dream.

At least once a week she got together with Mitch and Katie and Mr. McNulty. They talked one afternoon outside the McNulty's back gate, at the spot where Mr. Peabody had sent them traveling to the forest-lake. A breeze cooled the air and blew twirled patterns through the grasses on the hillside.

"So, the phone rings yesterday," Mr. McNulty said, "and it's Spongwell—Principal Spongwell, at Esterhaus. He's talking like the cheeriest guy you'd ever met. 'Hey, George! Long time no see! What's up?' Like he'd forgotten he fired me eight months ago. So we chat for a while like old pals, then he gets to business. There's this 'hot new trend' he's heard about, other schools are jumping in and he thinks it'll be big: *classical education*. Can you believe it? A *trend*, he called it. He says, 'I'm serious, George. People want to hear about all those old guys who wrote in Latin, like Homer and Plato." Mr. McNulty rolled his eyes and Mitch laughed, though Jessica wasn't sure why.

"Tell them the rest of it, George," Katie said.

Mr. McNulty shrugged. "Bottom line, he's looking to start a Classical Ed department next semester. He wants me to come back and run it."

"Oh, wow, seriously?" Mitch said.

"That's so cool!" Jessica said. "That would be great!"

Mr. McNulty grunted. "It's pointless. Twenty kids would sign up, maybe. Half of 'em would quit when they saw the workload."

"So, then you'd have the best kids in the school," Mitch said. He didn't look convinced. "Won't last a year before they go on to the next fad."

"Yeah, but it would be a great year," Mitch said.

"Come on, you've got to do it," Jessica said. "I was going to ask my Mom to take me out of Esterhaus. I'd stay for sure if you were there."

He shrugged again. "Well, it's just talk. I'm meeting Spong-well next week, probably I'll tell him to forget it." Then Katie caught Jessica's eye with a half-smile; it seemed to say, *Wait and see.*

On Sunday in that same week, Jessica came home after spending time with Mitch in the afternoon. She found her mother sitting on the couch, one hand holding the telephone handset and the other wiping at dampness on her cheeks. Before she could speak her mother straightened and said, "It was Brad—he just called! He's all right!"

Jessica made a sound like a shriek and jumped to the couch and they were both talking at once. Brad sounded tired but otherwise not horrible—he'd had rough times but said he was feeling better—didn't say anything about coming home—he was living in a large city but didn't say which one—he hoped he could see them but wasn't sure when.

"He asked about you," her mother said. "He had some kind of dream and somehow he got to thinking we might be worried. Can you imagine? Two years and *we might be worried!* Unbeliev-able. What's wrong with that boy?"

"I don't know, I wish I knew," Jessica said. "But I don't care. It's so great we know he's okay! Maybe sometime he'll think about coming back."

"Well, don't hold your breath." She let out a relaxing sigh. "Oh, Lord, but it's such a relief. Such a load off, I can't tell you."

"Same with me. Sometimes I hurt just thinking about him. Some nights I can't sleep and I lie there wondering where he is, or I pretend I can hear him moving around in his room, just to make me feel better."

Her mother gave Jessica a push in the shoulder. "You never tell me these things! You're so quiet all the time!"

"Yeah. Too quiet, I guess."

"Listen, now," she said, taking Jessica's hand, "I think about your brother and I get torn up inside—so much I should have done different. I don't ever want to feel that way about you."

Jessica squeezed her hand. "I'm not like him, Mom. I'd never run off like that."

"I know it. But can't we talk once in a while? You're too much like me, you clam up when the world gets on your back. But I was twelve once, I learned stuff the hard way, and you don't have to make *all* the same mistakes I did. You could skip a few of them, maybe?"

Jessica nodded. "Yeah, I'd like to talk more. Let's do that."

If nothing else had happened in those first weeks, Jessica wouldn't have complained or asked for more. But there was one other change, a quiet understanding she never spoke about to anyone.

She still had the stone Hunter gave her. She kept it in a dresser drawer with other keepsakes, except on the days when she carried it with her, nestled in a deep pocket of her jacket. Sometimes at night when the moon brightened her window, she brought it out and held it in her left hand, resting on the scar. She would think about two things Hunter said to her, still clear in her mind long after she'd returned.

He called her *daughter*. And he said, *You've done well.* Of all the things she'd seen and heard in the traveling, nothing seemed more important than those few words. Some days she could sense them dwelling in her like an inner warmth or a secret no one could see, and after feeling so confused for so long she wondered if she'd finally found, at least for a while, a place to rest.

. . .

On a Saturday morning in December not long before Christmas, Jessica and Mitch went out to the backyard of her townhouse. The day had started cold with heavy clouds rolling from the west and rain had been forecast for the afternoon, the first rain since April. The yard could certainly use it. Most of the grass had died during the parched summer and fall, leaving stiff patches of dried weeds. The only living plant was an orange tree in a back corner near a rusted swing set that no one had used in years.

"Hope this works," Mitch said.

Jessica smiled. "What, you worried?"

"Nah. Or just a little. But risks for research are OK. If it works, it might start answering some questions."

"Yeah. And if it doesn't...."

"I guess that'll be interesting too. So let's just do it."

From a pocket in her coat Jessica brought out the gift Ariel had given her, still in its wrapping. She pulled off the string and the brown paper. Inside, just as she'd known, was a small set of pipes—two wooden tubes carved and tied together by hand; they had been cut and holed to play a single chord. Jessica blew in them lightly and the familiar notes whistled in the air.

"So, what do we do?" Mitch said.

"First you have to hold my hand."

"Ewwwww!"

"Just do it, dummy."

"Okay, fine. Now what?"

"We close our eyes and run, and you have to think of a tree, a green tree. Then I blow on the pipes and we both jump."

Mitch breathed out through his teeth. "Okay. Here goes nothing."

They closed their eyes and ran and Jessica pictured the

green tree. She brought up the pipes and blew the chord, and they both jumped—

—and for the very first time, she began to understand. The tones sang from the pipes but not only from the pipes: she felt them rising from her lungs and her blood and her heart, felt her whole body—her whole *self*—tremble like a singing reed. At the same moment other sounds came to her, a music as vast as a gulf between worlds. Weaving through it she heard a familiar theme—her chord harmonized with it but wasn't quite on key. She altered the tones, tuning them with a twist in her gut; and then she moved, like an echo crossing a void, like fingers sliding down a scale—

—and both feet landed on firm earth. She breathed and smelled sweet wild air, rich with a hundred grasses and wildflowers. She opened her eyes and blinked against the green of the hills and the brilliant blue overhead.

It was the Summer Country, the first world Ariel had shown her, still so beautiful she could hardly bear to see it. The grass flowed away in sweeping folds of green, running down into hollows and rising into distant hills, striped with strands of trees that flowered yellow and orange. The wind lifted her hair and rippled the fields and rolled the clouds like white mountains across the sky.

Mitch shouted "*Wahoo!*" beside her, pumping his fists in the air. "You did it! You did it! Omigosh, omigosh!" Jessica yelled too and dropped backwards in the grass, arms stretched over her head, soaring inside like the clouds in the arching blue.

I get it now, she thought. *I know what you were trying to tell me.*

An art, a dance, an improvisation—that was the core of the traveling. In all of their guessing about it they had missed the essential truth: the primal music, the grand symphony and chorus that sang unending through the worlds. Somehow, all on her own, Ariel had learned to hear what no one else could hear. She'd heard it and found the skill to join it, tuning herself like an instrument, riding the themes wherever they would take her.

I can't see everything you've seen. I can't create like you do. But I can copy you, and that's enough. Until you come back and teach me some more.

Mitch practically bounced with excitement. "You gotta tell me about the traveling. But not now. Which way to the big hill?"

"That way," Jessica said, pointing as she got up. Mitch took off running and Jessica came after. In hardly any time at all they had drawn long tracks through the waving grass.

Mitch cupped his hands and yelled, "Thank you, Ariel!"

"Hurry back!" Jessica called. "We miss you!" Then she quit talking and doubled her speed. Because whatever else happened, she was *not* going to let Mitch win this race.

About the Author

David E. Gaston began writing stories at a very early age, with an enthusiasm that may have annoyed his parents and siblings more than he realized. At university he found that some instructors were surprisingly open to receiving a short story as a final project in place of an essay or report. His first published work was "Alisia's Gift" (*Amazing Stories*, March 1986). For many years he worked as a designer and writer of award-winning interactive learning experiences, while developing storylines for the novels that begin with *Songweaver Lost*.

He and his wife Carrie live on a micro-farm in Southern California with a few chickens, many native plants, and occasional possums and raccoons.

Visit us at davidegaston.com.

9 780961 793418